HIS STRANGE
WAYS

HIS STRANGE WAYS

Robin Hardy

Westford Press

His Strange Ways
Contemporary Christian fiction/allegory
2nd edition

ISBN: 978-1-934776-77-3

Westford Press
mail@westfordpress.com

This is a work of fiction. Only one character is intended to bear resemblance to a living person; all other resemblances to other persons, living or dead, are coincidental.

Cover image of Dallas TX © 2006 Troy Heerwagen, http://troyh.us

Amy Carmichael, *Gold Cord: The Story of a Fellowship* (London: SPCK, 1957).

The verses in Chapter 6 are excerpts from Job 10, taken from the HOLY BIBLE, NEW INTERNATIONAL VERSION. NIV. Copyright 1973, 1978, 1984 by International Bible Society. Used by permission of Zondervan Publishing House. All rights reserved.

The descriptions of document seals in Chapter 7 are from P.D.A. Harvey and Andrew McGuinness, *A Guide to British Medieval Seals* (Toronto: University of Toronto Press, 1996), pp. 48-49.

Virgil, *The Aeneid*, translated by Robert Fitzgerald (New York: Vintage Books, 1990). The quotations are from pp. 17, 3, 169-70, 304.

Heather Smith Thomas, *Storey's Guide to Raising Beef Cattle* (North Adams, MA: Storey Publishing, 1998).

Doris Herold Lund, *Attic of the Wind* (New York: Parents' Magazine Press, 1966).

I have no knowledge to take up the Lord, in all his strange ways and passages of deep and unsearchable providence; for the Lord is before me, and I am so bemisted that I cannot follow him: He is behind me, and following at the heels, and I am not aware of him: He is above me, but his glory so dazzleth my twilight of short knowledge, that I cannot look up to him: He is upon my right hand, and I see him not;

*H*e is upon my left hand, and within me, and goeth and cometh, and his going and coming are a dream to me: He is round about me, and compasseth all my goings, and still I have him to seek: He is every way higher, and deeper, and broader, than the shallow and ebb handbreadth of my short and dim light can take up; and therefore I would my heart could be silent, and sit down in the learnedly ignorant wondering at that Lord, whom men and angels cannot comprehend. . . .

O never-enough admired Godhead, how can clay get up to thee? How can creatures of yesterday be able to enjoy thee?

Samuel Rutherford
to the Laird of Carletoun
May 10, 1637

1

Finally alone, Paul sat, elbows on his knees, hands clasped, in the elegant front room of the Grayson Homestead. He halfheartedly listened as the surviving homeowner, Jeannine, ushered out the last of the mourners: "Thank you. I do thank you so for coming, and the casserole was wonderful. Are you sure you don't want the leftovers? All right, then, it will get eaten. . . .

"No, really, I'm quite all right. Yes, I was sorry that we couldn't get hold of Buddy. I understand that he and his wife are somewhere in the Caribbean right now, but he loved his father and he'll come as soon as he gets the message."

There were some protestations, and Paul detected a trace of weary desperation as she insisted, "No, please, there's not a thing more you can do. Yes, I certainly will call. Thank you again. Have a good flight back."

He heard the front door close, then a moment later Jeannine dragged herself in and plopped onto the hard formal sofa beside him. He turned to eye her in companionable suffering. "I thought you might have to dynamite them out," he observed.

Jeannine expelled a tired laugh, then insisted, "The Brodericks are good people—they'd do anything to help you. They just can't stand to miss out on any drama." She daubed at her eyes again, looking suddenly older than her 54 years. "Well." She straightened, smoothing her short frosted bob, then smiled gamely and rested a light hand on Paul's clenched hands. "Thank you."

"Don't start on me; I live here," he retorted.

She laughed. "Paul, I mean it. I don't know what I would have done without you."

He groaned, falling back on the stiff cushion. He was thirty-six, tan and lean, with unremarkable features and dark brown hair that tended to hang in his eyes. "Lot of good I did Walt."

She bit her lip, still resting a hand on his. "If you hadn't seen it happen, we wouldn't have found him for a day or two."

Head back, he removed his hand from under hers to cover his stinging eyes. "I should've insisted we wait on treating the foot rot. He had no business out there in this heat." August in Texas was guaranteed to be broiling.

"Don't *you* start. You know good and well that he was doing exactly what he wanted to. Dr. Cargyle said he could've had that heart attack just as well sitting in front of the TV," she said.

"Yeah," he exhaled, staring off into space.

A few minutes of silence followed—something rarely heard over the past three days. A young maid appeared at the entry: "Mrs. Ferring? I, um, finished the upstairs baths and the kitchen—"

"You can go, Shana. I know how much I've worked you this week," Jeannine said.

"Thank you, ma'am. Mr. Arrendondo," she nodded.

"Shana," he acknowledged, and she left.

He continued to lean his head back against the sofa, staring up at the ornate tiles on the thirty-foot-high ceiling. "Joe Salinas wants to buy the herd. He was going to try to make it out today to look them over."

She blinked. "I don't suppose you could handle them yourself, if we hired help . . . ?"

"No, Jeannine," he said. "I can't do what Walt did. I don't know how he did it for so long."

"And Buddy wouldn't want to," she murmured. That short sentence covered a wide disappointment, in that her son had always worked the ranch unwillingly with his father; when Paul came, Buddy took that for liberation and left. Guilt induced him back for a few months each year—until his marriage last summer.

Jeannine straightened in resolve. "Well, then, I'm sure Joe will give us a fair price for them."

Paul stirred uneasily at her use of the plural pronoun. The fact that he was still good friends with Buddy, and had worked for Walt on and off for six years now, gave him no formal standing in this family. Nor did he wish to —*formalize* anything here.

A long silence followed as he struggled with what to say. Finally, he murmured, "I'll stay long enough to see that the herd is transferred to Joe."

She quickly looked at him. "Paul, you can't leave." He closed his eyes. "When Royce comes back—"

He interrupted: "She isn't coming back; she's been gone almost a month now, Jeannine. That's what women do: they walk out on me." His first wife, Kris, had left him for another man. He and Royce had been married for a little over a year when she left in mid-July.

"It's not anything you did, Paul," she argued. "Royce just—needed to get back to the city for a little while." Living on a ranch, even one so luxurious, *was* an adjustment for a native New Yorker.

"A four-week vacation," he snorted. "Besides, at this point, what makes you think I'd take her back? She hasn't called; she won't pick up when I call."

Jeannine looked down. "What if she can't?" she asked quietly. "You don't know what has happened." He grunted skeptically, but his eyes were troubled when he looked through the large window to the rolling grassland in the afternoon light.

To his relief, he did not have long to ponder the question. Jesse, the Ferrings' hired hand, stepped into the doorway to tell them that Joe Salinas had arrived. Paul, still in his suit, went out to meet him with outstretched hand: "Joe! Glad you could make it."

"Hey, Paul." Brown, habitually smiling Joe gripped his hand. "Sorry I wasn't here for the funeral, Jeannine," he said to her. Without turning around, Paul could feel her at his back.

"That's all right, Joe; we wouldn't have had a chance to talk at all till now. Well. You want to have a look at them?" She gestured to the barbed-wire fence, behind which a few Red Angus could be seen.

"Sure," Joe allowed, and the three of them headed toward the fence while the visible cows watched suspiciously. "The gate's where?" Joe asked, as two of his employees fell in behind them.

"There." Paul pointed to their right. "It's unlatched."

Extracting a pen, pad, and calculator from his shirt

pocket, Joe nodded to his employees. They entered the pasture to examine a few of the herd. "Okay, then. How many head you got here?" Joe flipped open his pad.

Jeannine looked questioningly at Paul. "One hundred twelve," he replied.

"Oh. Lot less than when I was here last."

"Yeah," Paul said despondently.

So Joe went on to ask how many there were specifically of bulls, cows, yearlings, and calves, which Paul answered off the top of his head. "Um hmm. Um hmm." Joe noted the figures on his pad.

A few minutes later, his employees returned from a cursory inspection of the herd, and one whispered in Joe's ear. "You don't say," Joe muttered. Jeannine and Paul glanced at each other.

Whereupon Joe opened his calculator, entered a few figures, and said, "Well, then. Given their condition, and what all, I'm prepared to offer you sixty-eight thousand for the lot."

Jeannine looked to Paul for his reaction. "Is that a good price, Paul?"

He cleared his throat, glancing away. "Yeah, Jeannine. It's—probably the best you're gonna do, under the circumstances."

"Then it's a deal, Joe," she said.

Whereupon he pulled out a worn leather checkbook from his back jeans pocket and wrote out a check for that amount on the spot. He carefully tore it at the perforations, leaving a smudge on it as he handed it to her. "There you go, Jeannine. Now, you don't worry about a thing from here on out—we'll get them ready to transport and get the trucks out here."

"Fine, Joe," she murmured, holding the check.

He shook Paul's hand again, then went to his truck, extracting his phone from his pocket. As Paul turned back toward the house, he loosened his tie. "I'm . . . going to change." Jeannine nodded in response, accompanying him as far as the front foyer. From there, she went back to her office and he went up the stairs to his room on the second floor.

He shut the door and shucked his coat off onto the bed, then stood looking out the window with glassy eyes. San Angelo was just a few miles away, but from this window not even the highway was visible.

Paul remembered when, at Buddy and Renetta's wedding last June, Royce had gotten it into her head that he wasn't going to marry her after he'd already proposed. So without a word to him, she left the reception with a con artist who told her he was taking her to San Angelo. Of course, he didn't; he took her to Big Bend, and Joe Salinas had to bring her back. But since Paul had gone after her, and was not at the house when she got here, she bolted again.

"She's so gullible!" Paul muttered, exasperated. "She's always getting spooked and running! If she'd just settle down—" It occurred to him to wonder what he had done to spook her into leaving for a month.

Heaving a sigh, he opened his cell phone and looked at the number display. Once again, he clicked on her number and put the phone to his ear. It had been several weeks since he last attempted to call.

But this time, after the ring, he heard, "The number you have reached is temporarily out of service. We're sorry for the inconvenience."

Disquieted, Paul closed the phone. Had she changed her number? Lost the phone? Not paid her bill? Her phone was an older model, like his, and their plan did not provide many bells and whistles, like internet access.

He fell back onto the bed and stared up at the ceiling. Again, he was at a familiar impasse: he knew he needed to pray, but he just couldn't bring himself to do it. As long as he felt that God was jerking him around, he couldn't swallow his pride enough to go crawling back for help. Was that it? *Yep, that's pretty much why.*

He couldn't shake the feeling that God was playing with him out of spite. Paul knew, theoretically, that it wasn't so, and he knew the warped impressions left on him by a stern theological upbringing that said, *God does what He wants whether it makes any sense to you, you pitiful lump of clay, and you have nothing to say about it either way.* But knowing that his premises might be faulty did not enable him to change them.

There was a knock on his door; Paul sat up. "Yeah?"

Jeannine leaned her head in. "There's a lot of ham and dressing left over. I'm going to freeze most of it, but I thought you might want some before I do."

"Sure," Paul nodded. What he heard her saying was, *"There's no one else here and I don't want to eat alone"*—for which he really couldn't blame her. He just wished she had allowed a few of the many friends and relatives to stay so that he wouldn't have to fill the role of chief comforter. "Let me finish changing and I'll be right down."

"All right, then." She closed the door.

Paul got off the bed and whipped out his phone again, taking it to the attached bath. He selected Buddy's number from the list and put the phone to his ear. When Buddy's voice mail came on—again—Paul hissed, "Listen, a—hole, your mom needs you and I want you to get out here yesterday!" He snapped the phone shut and tossed it back onto the bed, then he sat on the closed toilet to take off his dress shoes.

After changing into jeans and t-shirt, Paul went downstairs to the spacious tiled kitchen with a bay window set in the breakfast nook. Jeannine glanced up from packing food into freezer containers. "I told as many people as I could collar not to bring anything, so I'm not sure how I wound up with all this." She gestured at a half-dozen casseroles ranging from hardly touched to mostly consumed.

"They all thought they were going to stay and eat what they brought," Paul said.

He reached under the sink for the topmost paper plate on a stack. "Oh, Paul, use a real plate," Jeannine chided.

"That I'll have to wash?" he said scornfully, spooning out dressing and sweet potatoes onto the paper plate.

She pushed the ham platter toward him, and he picked up a slice with his fingers to drop onto his plate. "Utensils are in the drawer to your left," she said archly.

"I know, Mom," he sighed.

"I'm too young to be your mother, remember?" she smiled, reciting his usual compliment.

"That you are," he agreed with the unsettling sensation of being tested.

He took his plate and utensils to the rattan table in the bay window. Jeannine opened the refrigerator. "I suppose you want one of your nasty beers."

He glanced up. "Sure. Thanks."

She brought it over to the table. "Do you want a glass?"

He eyed her. "Jeannine—"

"Teasing," she said, and he rolled his eyes.

She brought her plate (ceramic) and glass of iced tea to sit at the table with him. "Roger's still out of town," she noted as if continuing a conversation. Roger was the Ferring family lawyer. "So we won't see the will until he gets back. But I know Walt remembered you, Paul."

"I don't care, Jeannine," he muttered around a mouthful.

For a few minutes they ate in silence, then the telephone rang. Paul glanced up, taking a swig from the can, when she rose from the table to answer the kitchen extension. "Hello? Yes. Um, hold on, please." She lowered her voice to a whisper. "It's for you. It's Susan."

He looked blank. *Susan?* he mouthed.

"Buddy's sister-in-law," she whispered. He still looked blank. "Renetta's sister," she clarified.

Whereupon he recoiled, taking up his plate as if to flee. Jeannine replaced the receiver at her ear. "I'm sorry; he can't come to the phone right now. May I take a message? . . . All right, I will. Well—I'm not sure when he could call back. All right. Goodbye."

Jeannine reseated herself, so Paul did too, warily. "She just wanted to say hi and see how you're doing," she related.

Paul's face contorted in a mixture of incomprehension and revulsion. "I haven't seen her since Buddy and Renetta's wedding. Why would she—" His face cleared. "Renetta told her that Royce left me."

The phone rang again, and he got up from the table to stand in the doorway, prepared to run. Exhaling, Jeannine rose to answer it again: "Hello. Oh, Buddy! Finally! Where have you been?"

Listening, she brought the cordless handset to sit back down at the table, as did Paul. "Buddy, he had a heart attack three days ago. He and Paul were out in the upper pasture, and he just went down, Paul said. He— Paul—called nine-one-one and put him in the truck, but there was nothing anyone could do for him. Dr. Cargyle said he must have died instantly."

She took a bite of dressing as she listened, then brought the napkin up to her mouth. "I see. Yes, I understand what happens when you get in those dead spots. I'm sorry we couldn't hold the funeral any longer —yes, it was today. Um, yes, Buddy, I wish you'd come as soon as possible. Paul is leaving, and we need to discuss what to do about the ranch. Right. Love you too, honey. Bye." She clicked the phone off and set it down to continue eating.

Paul briefly struggled with curiosity before succumbing. "He couldn't call back because he was in a dead spot for three days?"

"He says he didn't get any messages before today. You never can tell, with international roaming," she insisted.

"Suppose so," he conceded. "When will he get here?"

"Tonight. They're on their way," she said.

They continued to eat. Gradually, it began to dawn on Paul that something was amiss. Jeannine loved her husband, but she was acting like no new widow that Paul ever knew. He shrugged, mentally, not eager to explore her feelings. Then he realized he'd better address it—at least find out why she was so cheerful, so to speak.

"Uh, Jeannine? I . . . I've got my hankie ready for the waterworks."

She eyed him, then smiled. "You're wondering why I'm not blubbering on your shoulder? I'm one of those people who grieve in private, Paul. I won't even cry in front of Buddy—I suppose it's a holdover from that 'strong pioneer spirit.' Besides which, if he had to die, it was the best way he could go. Quick and painless, doing what he loved."

"I'd agree with that," he nodded.

"Mostly, though, I don't think it's really hit me yet," she murmured. "I keep expecting him to appear at the back door, booming, 'Oh, hell! Take off the boots!'"

Paul ducked his head at the tears that suddenly spilled from his eyes. "Oh, Paul!" Jeannine whispered, and he waved it off, shame-faced.

Walt's death suddenly hit him like a wrecking ball. Having built his life around Walt, Paul was now left sitting on a pile of rubble. Even had he felt competent to continue to run the ranch as Walt did, his staying on in that capacity would provoke more gossip than he could deal with—only days ago he had overheard Shana on the phone speculating that Mrs. Arrendondo had left because Mr. Arrendondo was getting too cozy with Mrs. Ferring, which was ridiculous.

But the worst of it was, Jeannine's comment had triggered the realization that he, also, was expecting Walt to come stomping through the back door . . . and

Royce through the front door, tossing her purse on the kitchen counter as she always did. The finality of Walt's passing seemed to close the door on Royce's coming back, as well.

"I miss the old fart, too," Paul said to cover himself. He concentrated on finishing a plate of honey-baked ham that now tasted like straw.

Following the early dinner, he went to the den in the back of the house and turned on the TV. He wasn't looking for any particular show, but he had to do something to fill the quiet until Buddy arrived. Jeannine did not follow him back to the den, so he spread out on the couch to watch the baseball game between the Diamondbacks and the Astros, just getting underway.

Midway through the game, he thought he heard the front door open, so he raised the remote to mute the television. A moment later he faintly heard Jeannine talking to someone. Paul didn't bother to get up. A minute later, Buddy and Renetta came back to the den and sat down. "Hey," Buddy greeted him, and Paul nodded, eyes on the TV.

"I, uh, got my phone messages all at once when we got to Santo Domingo." Buddy, 32, had close-cropped, curly hair and a jawline that looked especially chiseled when he was tense, as now. His wife Renetta, a year younger, sat on the couch across from Paul and fixed him with large gray eyes. Her black hair had been professionally straightened and trimmed to fall just above her shoulders.

"Yeah," Paul muttered, aware that Jeannine had come to stand in the doorway.

Buddy added, "What's up with the herd?"

Paul clicked off the television. "C'mon out and I'll show you." He could have related the situation without taking Buddy outside, but he wanted to get out of the women's hearing—well, specifically, Renetta's.

He didn't dislike her, and he certainly didn't hold any grudges from her accidentally shooting him in the gut, but—he did kind of resent the way she had so thoroughly taken Buddy out of his life. Paul hardly ever saw him anymore.

So they two went out through the back door and crossed fifty feet of lawn to the gate of the pasture. A path had been worn by Walt years ago coming back and forth from the house to the pasture this way.

Reaching the gate, Paul leaned on it, looking over the shadowy heads of cattle in the evening darkness. "Okay, well, they're off their feed, and foot rot's going around. Joe offered Jeannine sixty-eight thou for the lot, and I recommended she accept it. She did. He's trucking them out probably tomorrow."

"Sixty-eight—!" Buddy sputtered. "For more than a hundred thirty head?"

Paul glanced at him. "There's only a hundred twelve now, Buddy. Walt just couldn't keep up with them like he used to, and he won't hire help. He doesn't—didn't— trust anybody but me and Jesse to work with them."

"Why wouldn't you stay on, Paul?" Buddy asked, with a glance back to the house. His mother's silhouetted figure could be seen in a window.

Paul sagged on the gate. "I couldn't, not with Royce gone."

"What—" Buddy shifted to lower his voice. "What happened with her? She just upped and left?"

"Kinda," Paul muttered. "We had another fight. She just . . . couldn't get used to down time on a ranch. Jeannine . . . must have noticed that something was wrong with Walt. He wouldn't go in for a checkup, or anything, of course, so she slowed down her work schedule quite a bit to be home more, until it seemed like she wasn't going anywhere. She stopped lecturing, and stepped down as chair of the symphony fund-raiser.

"Royce was supposed to be her assistant, you know, and so all of a sudden she didn't have anything to do, and the last straw was when I suggested she get a job at a dress shop in San Angelo. She hit the roof— 'I'm going back to the city!' and she hitched a ride with Patricia into town.

"Who knows where she went from there—nobody's seen her in San Angelo. So, I call her cell about three days later, and she wouldn't pick up. Last time I tried to call, her number was out of service," Paul shrugged.

Buddy was silent for a while. "That doesn't sound like Royce. Something must have happened to her. Have you called the police?"

Paul blew a scornful raspberry: "She's twenty-six, which is an adult anywhere. I call the police, they're most likely to start investigating me for murder."

"Well—have you gotten any of her mail?" Buddy asked.

"No, nothing," Paul said.

"No credit-card statements that might tell you where she's spending money?" Buddy pressed.

"No. I know she had at least one card, but. . . ."

"Does she have any of your cards?" Buddy asked.

"I gave her one a long time ago, which she used

exactly once. And I just checked my statement online day before yesterday—there are no charges that aren't mine," Paul said.

"Something's wrong, Paul," Buddy insisted. "Have you tried calling her parents?"

Paul rounded on him. "Were you there when her mother Sue Anne shredded me at our first meeting? After thirty minutes of pounding me into mincemeat, she turned around and left again."

"So? Why are you just rolling over and playing dead?" Buddy asked.

"Why should I do anything to get her back? That relationship is so *yesterday*, guy," Paul sneered, imitating Renetta's New York friends. "I can accept it when something's over."

"You owe it to her to at least find out if she's okay!" Buddy snapped.

That hit home, and Paul lifted a hand from the gate in resignation. "I don't know where to start. New York City's a big place."

"Her parents still live there, don't they?" Buddy asked. "Start there."

"They're not going to talk to me," Paul stated.

"Then maybe they'll talk to Ren. She and Royce are friends; they used to work at the same company. Do you have their number?"

"Why would I—" Paul broke off, suddenly extracting his phone. He murmured, "You know, she did use my phone for a while when hers was on the fritz, and she might have put her dad's number—yeah, there it is: 'Daddy.' She put her dad's number in my address book. Lowell Lindel."

"He'd talk to you, wouldn't he?" Buddy asked.

"For all I know, it's their home phone number, and if I call, Sue Anne is guaranteed to answer."

"Then we'll get Ren to call." Buddy turned back toward the house, and Paul followed.

They reentered the den, where Renetta and Jeannine looked up from the couch. "'Scuse me, Mom, we need to borrow Ren," Buddy said. Jeannine nodded, and Renetta rose to go with the men into the study. Buddy closed the door and turned to his wife. "Honey, we need a favor. Would you call this number—?"

"—on your phone, so my name won't show up," Paul interrupted.

"Yeah," Buddy said, gesturing to her purse. "It's Royce's dad. Would you call and ask him where she is?"

Paul objected, "Actually, it'd probably go over better if you just ask to talk to her."

"Yeah," Buddy agreed. Throughout this interchange, Renetta was glancing back and forth between them.

"Of course," she said. She set her purse on a nearby desk and took out her phone. Paul held his up so that she could see the number for "Daddy." This she dialed, and put the phone to her ear.

Shortly, she straightened. "Hello, this is Renetta Cleary Ferring. I worked with Royce at The Chocolate Conglomerate, and I was trying to get in touch with her. Is she there, please?"

2

*B*uddy and Paul stood close by on either side of Renetta as she listened over her cell phone. Paul could barely discern the voice on the other end, so he couldn't tell whether it was Royce's father or not. "I see," Renetta said. "I will. Thank you very much."

With pressed lips and raised brow, she terminated the call. "I assume it was her dad who answered, but he didn't say. He did say that Royce called about three weeks ago from Fort Worth, and he hasn't heard from her since, so, whenever I do get hold of her, he would like to hear from her, as well."

Buddy looked quickly at Paul, who glanced away, muttering, "I don't know why she'd go to Fort Worth."

"That's where you're from," Buddy observed.

"So? That can't be why she went," Paul objected.

Buddy retorted, "You're just full of excuses. Are you really going to stand there and tell me you're not going to find out what happened to her?"

Paul dropped his head. "No. I'll go." Turning, he saw the shadow of feet pass from the other side of the closed door.

He found Jeannine in the kitchen. He cleared his throat upon approaching, to give her the opportunity to act surprised that he was there. "Jeannine, um . . . Ren got hold of Royce's dad, who said the last time he heard from her was three weeks ago. She called from Fort Worth, so . . . I'm going to see if I can find her. I'll be leaving first thing in the morning."

"You and she are welcome back any time, Paul," she said.

"Thank you, Jeannine. I'm . . . very grateful for everything you and Walt did for me, opening your home to me, and giving me a job, and welcoming Royce. . . ."

"Well then, be sure to let me know when you find her," she said.

"I will," he smiled feebly. The moment cried out for a hug, but he was too afraid to risk it, even with Buddy and Renetta in the house. "Good night, Jeannine."

"Paul," she nodded.

Before seven o'clock the following morning, Paul had two bags packed and loaded in his red Chevy truck. It clearly looked, and smelled, like a ranch vehicle, but in Fort Worth, home of the Stockyards, it would blend right in, as long as he stayed out of his brother Ed's posh suburban neighborhood. If anything like this truck was ever spotted in Westover Hills, it had better be pulling a trailer full of yard maintenance equipment.

Technically, the truck was Walt's, but Paul had used it, maintained it, and repaired it for so long that the whole household referred to it as "Paul's truck." In the back of his mind, he resolved to pay Jeannine for it, so that he could get title to it before the next insurance payment was due. But because he knew she'd want to give it to him when he asked, he wanted to be able to put a check in her hand for it, and right now he had less than $400 in his bank account.

The "substantial" reward that the DEA was going to pay for his services as guide in Big Bend turned out to be only $5000, which he promptly blew on a diamond ring for Royce. Thereafter, she demonstrated a startling ability to spend everything they both earned, even given their nominal living expenses, before deciding she needed the greater spending venues of a big city.

Fort Worth, Paul groaned. *Why would she go there?* Must be because it was the closest big city she had a glancing knowledge of. Unfortunately, it was also where his parents lived. He still sent his mother money, and would continue to do so, but he wanted nothing to do with his father. And after Royce's one and only meeting with him, Paul was sure she felt the same. So whatever support she was looking for there, it wasn't to be found in them.

Sliding behind the wheel of the truck, Paul set his sunglasses on his face and started the ignition, then shifted into gear to turn down the long gravel drive to the white gate.

The airport, he suddenly realized. *Dallas/Fort Worth International*. She could go anywhere in the world from there. Paul lurched to a dead halt in the middle of the drive. His truck died; after a moment, he restarted the engine and proceeded onto the dirt road leading to the highway. Turning onto Highway 277 north, he grimly settled in for the four-hour drive to Fort Worth.

Along the way, Paul thought over his options. He glanced at his watch, then picked up his phone from the seat beside him. Keeping an eye on sparse highway traffic, he scrolled through the directory until he came to "Daddy" again. He pressed the call button and put the phone to his ear.

"Hello?"

"Ah, Mr. Lindel? This is Paul Arrendondo. I—apologize for calling so early—"

"That's all right. I'm just sitting in traffic."

"Ah, good. Me, too." Paul cleared his throat. "Um, Renetta told me she had called you, and I was hoping to get a little more information. When, ah, when Royce called, what did she tell you? Did she say she was going anywhere?"

Several seconds of silence. "Is there a problem between you?"

"Frankly, Mr. Lindel, I don't know. Royce left, and then called you, and nobody's heard from her since. I just want to know that she's all right—"

"I'm calling the police," Lowell said, and clicked off.

"Well, my plan is unfolding beautifully, so far," Paul remarked, replacing the phone on the passenger seat. He half expected it to ring back with a call from the FBI, but as minutes passed and the phone stayed quiet, he forgot about it to concentrate on the suddenly heavy traffic. He exited to I-20 in Abilene, merging with the surging wall of Friday morning traffic headed toward Fort Worth.

As he approached the outlying suburbs, a gentle suggestion crossed his mind. He ignored it, given the task at hand. When he was passing through the suburbs in south Fort Worth, the suggestion returned less gently. He considered it, then again rationalized it away.

But when he approached the turn-off to his parents' part of town, the suggestion emerged as a shouted mandate, and he yielded with a groan. He stopped at an ATM for cash, but instead of the fifty or hundred he usually withdrew for his mother, today he took out two hundred, bringing his balance dangerously low.

With sinking heart, he cruised the old neighborhood of potholed streets and shotgun houses—long, narrow shanties in which you could (theoretically) stand at the front door and fire a shotgun so that the blast passed through every room of the house and on out the back. Some of these houses were really nice when first built, back in the 1920s or so. Now, they were crumbling.

Paul pulled up into the grassless yard of one such house and cut the engine. The neighborhood was strangely quiet—there was usually a group of unemployed or truant boys wandering around looking for trouble. He emerged from the truck, frowning at the orange paper flapping on the front door of his parents' home.

Hopping up the collapsed concrete steps, he ripped the paper off the door, tucking his sunglasses into his shirt pocket. "This is—Mama! Mama?" He opened the rusty screen, peering into the dingy front room. "Mama?" He went on into the next room, the kitchen, which was dim and still. With no air conditioning, it was also stiflingly hot. But he heard sounds from the room beyond that, and poked his head through the doorway.

The window was open, but the shade was drawn and the other door shut, preventing any appreciable air circulation. Paul's mother looked up from her chair at his father's bedside. "Oh, Paul! He's not feeling well." She was attempting to bathe her husband's forehead with cool, wet cloths.

"Mama, there was a demolition notice on the door! The city is going to—" He broke off to stare down at his father, whose thin body shuddered with heaving gasps. "What—" Stuffing the paper into a pocket, Paul sank to his knees beside the bed. He grasped his father's wrist to feel the faint, rapid pulse, then reached over to lift an eyelid enough to see a large pupil. "Mama, you've got to call an ambulance," he said, pulling out his phone, as there was none in this house.

She looked at him inquiringly. "Paul? What's wrong with Papa?"

"He—" Paul snapped the phone shut upon realizing that no ambulance would find its way to an unmarked house on an unmarked street in time to do his father any good. "We have to get him to the hospital," he said, throwing the old man's arm over his shoulder and hoisting him.

"What, Paul?" she said anxiously.

He put his mouth close to her ear to shout, "He has to go to the hospital! Help me get him into the truck!"

"Oh, no, Paul; Papa hates hospitals. He won't go," she said dolefully.

"He doesn't have any choice," Paul grunted.

With his mother following, clucking in anxious disapproval, Paul trotted out of the house carrying his father. He stopped at the truck's passenger door, nodding, "Open it!"

She did, and he slid the limp man onto the bench

seat. "Hurry, Mama!" He grabbed her elbow to assist her in and shut the door.

Scampering around the front, he slid behind the wheel and started the ignition. As he put the truck into gear, he looked down at the sudden moisture on his leg, and saw that his father had evacuated—not a good sign. Setting his jaw, Paul whipped the truck onto the narrow street and gunned it toward the nearest hospital. He hoped to pick up a cop on the way to get him through red lights, but he was careening up to the hospital's emergency entrance before he saw any.

Cutting the engine, he turned to look at his father resting in his mother's arms. She held him tenderly, childlike; being stouter than he, she easily enveloped his bony frame with her arms. But Paul looked at the lax jaw, the half-closed eyes, the still chest, and knew that they were too late.

A hospital orderly opened the passenger door; Paul's mother climbed out to allow him to lift out her husband onto a waiting gurney and rush him inside. Paul restarted the truck to move it so as not to block the emergency drive-through, then got out. After pausing to assess the smelly brown stain on his jeans, he accompanied his mother into the waiting room.

They were directed to a semi-cubicle where a smiling woman sat behind a computer monitor. "Good morning. Oops, I see that we're just past noon now. Name?"

Paul seated his mother, then heavily sat himself. "That is my father, Rafael Arrendondo, who was just brought in. This is my mother Juanita Arrendondo. I am Paul Arrendondo."

After making sure she had the spellings correct, the clerk entered the information on her computer. "Address?"

Paul paused, feeling the orange demolition notice in his pocket. Then he went ahead and gave that address. His mother watched closely, being unable to hear anything that was transpiring.

"All right. Insurance information?" the clerk asked hopefully.

Paul shook his head. "They have no insurance."

"Responsible party?" she asked, eyeing him.

"Me," he said.

"Address?" she inquired.

With minimal hesitation, Paul brought out his driver's license with the Ferrings' address. The clerk copied all information from that, then asked, "Place of employment?"

"The Ferrings'," he nodded at the driver's license she still held. "It's a ranch."

When she had extracted all information from him, she nodded him toward the waiting area. "Take a seat, please." Then she printed off a page and left.

By the time Paul had guided his mother to a chair, a white coat appeared at a doorway to call, "Arrendondo?"

Paul got his mother back up to meet the doctor, who gestured them inside a small consultation room. "Okay," he said uncomfortably, "ah, we're not getting any vitals, so we need to know how vigorously to attempt resuscitation."

"Don't," Paul said, shaking his head.

"What, Paul?" his mother cried.

He put his mouth to her ear. "He's dead. They want

to know how hard they need to try to bring him back."

"Yes!" she cried, turning to the doctor. "Yes, save him, *por favor*!" Having spoken English for the last forty years or so, she lapsed into Spanish only when she was very upset.

The doctor looked back at Paul. "This is his wife?"

"Yes, but I am his son," Paul said tensely.

The doctor turned to her and said, "*Intentaré, señora.*"

She gripped her son's arm. "What, Paul?"

He groaned, "Mama, Papa is gone—"

The doctor stopped him. "If she wants us to keep trying, we will. Please go have a seat."

Dismally, Paul took his mother back out to the waiting area. "What, Paul?" she asked again.

He inhaled, glancing around the half-full waiting room. So he stepped to the clerk and said, "We'll be right outside." Then he took his mother outside to the covered walkway and shouted, "Mama, he's old; he ready to die. Let him go."

"But how will I live, Paul?" Her brown eyes were large with fear.

"You've got five kids that are going to take care of you, Mama!" he shouted. A passer-by glanced at him, offended. "Come." Paul lowered his voice to a normal level and gestured her back inside.

They sat and waited for another hour or so, watching other patients being called into examining rooms. There were empty chairs all around Paul and his mother; anyone who sat near him quickly got up to sit elsewhere. Paul looked back and forth between the odorous stain on his leg and the sign for the men's restroom, but he was afraid to leave his mother alone in the waiting room, in case they called her name. At length, the same doctor came to the door; catching Paul's eye, he gestured. Paul urged his mother up and they followed him back to the consultation room. "I'm sorry," the doctor told Paul. "He did not respond to our resuscitation efforts."

Paul opened his mouth to utter a retort before realizing that the doctor was merely conveying information that he wished passed along to the widow. So Paul took his mother's hand, patted it, and shook his head. She fell into him, crying loudly.

"We need his social for the death certificate," the doctor said. "Which funeral home do you want to pick up the body?"

Paul exhaled in indecision, and the doctor said, "Please just give the information to the receiving clerk when you have it." Then he glanced down at the liquid excrement on Paul's leg that smelled very bad.

"Yes. Thank you," Paul said. He ushered his mother out to the truck. Opening the door of the hot cab, he gagged at the overpowering smell. "Wait here, Mama!"

"What?"

He gestured, "Wait! I'll be right back!" She nodded, and he hurried back into the waiting room, and from there to the men's restroom, where he grabbed a handful of paper towels. First, he dampened them with soap and water and cleaned his leg as best he could. Then he took a few soapy towels and a lot of dry ones out to his truck.

While his mother stood by, he cleaned the worst of the discharge off the seat and spread the dry towels over the rest. Juanita settled herself gingerly while he disposed of the soiled towels, then he drove back to the little house that had been her home for the last half-century. How she had ever raised five children here was one of those inexplicable mysteries of life.

Entering, Paul shouted, "Mama, I need you to find all yours and Papa's papers. All the important papers. Then you need to pack your good things. You have to leave the house."

"Leave? Why, Paul?" she asked.

He pulled out the crumpled city demolition notice, printed in both English and Spanish. "The house has been condemned. It's going to be torn down. I'll help you pack whatever you want to take."

She stared at the notice. "But . . . where will I go?"

"I'll find you a good place, Mama. I'll take care of you!"

She nodded reluctantly, and he gestured her to the back of the house.

Over the next two hours, he salvaged the cleanest boxes he could find from fast-food dumpsters and helped her pack her treasured little worthless knickknacks, her Bible and wrinkled devotional magazines, her shabby clothes, and all the paperwork he could locate. He consented to pick out his father's best suit for him to be buried in. But he absolutely drew the line at broken lamps, cracked dishes, and sagging furniture. Over and over, he promised, "I'll get you better stuff, Mama! You won't need any of this!"

Finally, with five boxes loaded in the bed of the pickup, Paul drove his teary mother from her old home for the last time. He bought a late lunch for them both from the drive-through of a Taco Bueno, and they sat to eat in the shade of a cheerful little park across the street from a shopping mall the size of a decent suburb. Stopping in a public restroom, he attempted again to clean his jeans, the smell of which was becoming intolerable in the heat. Then he drove back to the hospital.

He parked and sat his mother in the waiting room as before. She carried in, and insisted on handing over to him, the grocery sack containing his father's burial clothes.

This in hand, he approached the same admissions clerk. "I've . . . brought all the information I could find for Rafael Arrendondo." He extended his father's birth certificate (a treasured document proving his United States citizenship), his Social Security card, his long-expired driver's license, and a few other miscellaneous documents.

She looked up. "Oh, yes. Please have a seat." He sat while she flipped through the papers and entered all pertinent numbers from the deceased's life.

Following that, she printed off several pages from her computer. "Okay. Here's two copies of the death certificate—death was attributed to congestive heart failure." She tapped a whole stack of documents together to hand neatly to him, adding, "Death certificates are thirty-five dollars each."

Paul shifted to reach for his wallet, but she elaborated, "Oh, wait. They're included in the emergency room charges. The total cost for Mr. Arrendondo's emergency care is four thousand, one hundred seven dollars and sixty-eight cents." She tapped the topmost paper.

Paul was left gasping as he looked at the single sheet

of expenses, most of which were for resuscitation efforts, apparently. Even equipped with a master's degree (in divinity) he was unable to interpret the specific charges—except the last line, which was for two death certificates, $35 each. He shut his dry mouth, then reached into his back pocket for his wallet, from which he pulled out a credit card to hand over.

The clerk entered the information from the card, then handed it back. "All right! Now all we need to know is the name of the funeral home you want to pick up the body."

Paul sagged, glancing back at his mother trustfully waiting. "She has nothing to pay for a funeral with."

"Indigent burial is only a thousand dollars," the clerk told him. "Then the county takes care of everything."

Sinking ever lower, Paul re-extracted his wallet and flipped through it to hand her another credit card. She entered the information from this one, then returned it to him, along with a computer-generated receipt. "Okay! You'll be receiving a letter with the date and location of graveside services. Have a good day, now."

Nodding numbly, Paul rose. "Oh." He leaned down and picked up the sack containing his father's clothes. "Here is his burial suit."

She glanced up to take the sack, which she dropped at her feet. Paul did not doubt that from there, it would be deposited in the closest trash can. From his previous work with addicts, he knew that the county buried their indigents in body bags.

He collected his mother to escort her back out to his truck. She checked to make sure all the boxes were still there (as if any of it was worth stealing) then sat while he started the engine. He stuffed in her oversized handbag all documents that the clerk had given him, but she pulled back out the death certificate, setting dollar-store reading glasses on her nose to look it over carefully. "What about the funeral, Paul? Who do we see about that?"

He leaned close to her ear so that he didn't have to shout, only talk loudly: "The county is taking care of everything, Mama. They're going to tell us when and where it will be."

She accepted that with apparent relief. "Will you call your brother and sisters for me, to tell them?"

"Yes, Mama," he nodded. Turning the air conditioner to *high*, he sat and thought about that. His three sisters were spread all over Texas—he wasn't even sure he had current phone numbers for them. But his brother was here in Fort Worth. He shouted, "Do you know Ed's number?"

"Eddie? Eddie hasn't come by in a long time, Paul," she said resentfully.

"No, I guess not," he sighed, extracting his phone to call up directory assistance for the law firm at which his brother worked. This he dialed. At the receptionist's answer, he said, "I'm calling for Ed Arrendondo. This is his brother Paul, and it is urgent."

"One moment, please," she said, putting him on hold.

Several minutes later a cheerful male voice came on the line: "Hello?"

"Ed? This is Paul."

"Paul, you old bugger, how are you? Hey, I'm really six feet under here, so can I call you back in an hour?"

"Ed, Papa died."

"Oh, man, I'm sorry to hear that."

"Uh, yeah. His final care and costs for indigent burial came to over five thousand dollars," Paul mentioned.

"Uh huh," was all Ed said.

Paul stuttered, "I—I put all of it on my charge card. I'd appreciate you and the girls kicking in to help with that."

"Sure, buddy. No problem," Ed said. "Now, if you'll excuse me, I've got—"

"Ed," Paul interrupted, "Mama had to leave the house. It's been condemned. She needs a place to stay."

"Well, you always said you'd take her in," Ed pointed out.

Paul shifted the phone to his other ear. "Ed, I just left the Ferrings'. I'm not staying there anymore, and I don't have a new place yet. When I get one, I will bring her to live with me, but until then—can you just take her in until I get settled?"

Ed balked, "Oh, man, I don't know. Mandy's got her hands full with the girls' cheerleading squad, and all, and she's just so uncomfortable around Mom, being deaf and all. You'll have to let me talk it over with her and get back to you. But thanks for your call." And he clicked off.

3

*P*aul quietly closed the phone while his mother watched with inquisitive eyes. He leaned over to say in her ear, "He said he was very sorry."

"What's he going to do about it?" she said suspiciously. "His wife won't let him do anything," she answered herself.

Paul closed his eyes, then restarted the truck and pulled into a nearby gas station. Motioning his mother to wait, he filled the gas tank, paying with his rapidly diminishing credit. Then he climbed back into the cab, fingering the worn leather tag on his keyring. His mother settled herself, waiting. With a sigh of reluctance, he turned the wheel into Friday afternoon rush-hour traffic, heading south. There was only one thing he knew to do at this point, and it chafed him sorely to do it.

By the time they arrived at the Grayson Homestead, it was past nine o'clock, and dark out. But the security lights around the stately old mansion illumined it well to Juanita's widened eyes. "Paul," she said, her voice catching, "who lives here, in a place like this?"

Paul cut the engine to lean over to her. "Jeannine

Ferring! She just lost her husband, just like you, and she needs help! You can help her until I get back. Okay, Mama?" he pleaded.

She looked at him dubiously. "If it is okay with this Jeannie Fearing."

"Jeannine. Jeannine Ferring," he said loudly.

"I heard you," she said, offended. Paul sighed and climbed out to help her down from the cab.

Dry-mouthed, he led her up the steps to the carved double front doors. As many times as he had casually gone in and out through these doors, tonight, he reached for the doorbell. Juanita smoothed her dress self-consciously. Before Paul could ring the bell, the door swung open and he was staring into Jeannine's steady eyes. "Ah, Jeannine,—"

"Please come in," she said, stepping back.

Hesitantly, Paul brought his mother inside. She sidled into the foyer, glancing around the luxurious front rooms. Paul began again: "Jeannine, this is my mother, Juanita."

Buddy and Renetta suddenly appeared from a back room. His face opened in pleasant surprise and he shouted with the power and enunciation of an opera singer: "HELLO, MRS. ARRENDONDO! GOOD TO SEE YOU!" His mother stared at him.

"Hello, Buddy," Juanita said, flushing happily. "You look nice. Who is this?"

"THIS IS MY WIFE REN, MRS. ARREN-DONDO," Buddy replied, a hand at his startled wife's back.

"So nice to meet you," Juanita nodded. Renetta smiled and waved lightly.

Paul wiped his mouth. "Jeannine, my father died today, and their home is scheduled for demolition next Tuesday—"

"YOU STAY HERE, MRS. ARRENDONDO," Buddy broadcast to all of south Texas.

"Are you sure?" Juanita murmured in that thick voice of the deaf. Buddy, to everyone's gratitude, merely nodded vigorously. "I have some boxes in Paul's truck." She gestured timidly toward the door.

"Buddy," his mother said in a one-word instruction.

"Sure," he said. Renetta accompanied him out to fetch Juanita's entire worldly possessions.

Paul turned back to Jeannine. "I'll—come get her when I have a place to stay. I haven't had a chance to do anything else yet. Uh, she, she won't be a lot of trouble; she's a good worker, a great cook, and she—"

"Don't apologize for her, Paul," Jeannine said in rebuke as she took Juanita's arm. "Come have dinner." Gesturing to the open door of the kitchen, Jeannine made her meaning clear without having to shout.

Juanita accepted, asking, "Buddy is your son?" Jeannine nodded. "He is so nice," Juanita said approvingly.

Jeannine glanced back. "Would you like to wash up, Paul?"

"I can't stay, Jeannine—"

"You'll want to wash up before you leave," she said, without looking at his stained pants.

"Yes. Thank you," he exhaled in defeat.

He went out to get a suitcase while Buddy and Renetta brought in Juanita's boxes. Buddy stopped him to ask, "What happened?"

Paul muttered, "Just that—as soon as I got into Fort

Worth, I stopped in to see them. There was a demolition notice on the door, and Papa dying in the bedroom. I got him to the emergency room in time for them to perform four thousand dollars' worth of useless resuscitation on him."

"Ouch," Buddy said.

"So I wasted a whole day on that—"

"'Wasted'?" Renetta repeated in disbelief.

Paul gestured in frustration. "You know what I mean. I wasn't able to do a thing about Royce. I called her dad, and as soon as he realized I was trying to find her, he threatened to call the cops on me. Well—" he looked at his pants in exasperation—"I'm going to shower, then I'm out of here."

"Good luck," Buddy murmured, and Renetta (being short) squeezed Paul around the middle. He tried not to flinch, but she was pressing right where she had shot him. He'd not had that slug removed yet, and every now and then, it reminded him that it was still there.

Paul took a suitcase up to his old room, where he undressed. He regarded his jeans in disgust, then wadded them up into the trash can. After showering, he packed everything back in his suitcase and took it downstairs.

With some trepidation, he paused at the door of the kitchen. He didn't hear any shouting, only his mother's voice. So he looked in. A partially empty plate in front of her, she was apparently in the midst of reciting the Arrendondo Family History to Jeannine.

Seeing Paul in the doorway, she interrupted herself to ask, "Paul, did you call the Mount Zion Baptist Church about Papa's death? They will want to do something for his funeral."

"Uh, not yet, Mama, but I'm on my way back to Fort Worth, so I'll try to. . . ."

She had relocated her glasses from the top of her head to her nose in order to read from a legal pad on the table, where Jeannine was writing something. Juanita told her in evident reply, "That's where Papa—Rafe—worked from the first day he dropped out of high school. When Paul came along a few years later—he's our firstborn—the church was so good to us. They brought us diapers and formula, and groceries, so Rafe just worked his heart out for them. He did all the yard work, plumbing, building, roofing—anything that needed fixing, they just called Rafe and he did it, any time of day or night.

"Then he started with the heart trouble, oh, five, six years ago, and couldn't work anymore, so we heard no more from them. But they will want to know, Paul," she said, turning back to him. "Just call Pastor Blount."

"Yes, Mama," he said. Pastor Blount had left that church shortly before Rafael's heart trouble began, and Paul had no idea where he might be now.

Jeannine glanced back at Paul, then gestured to the platter of ham and dressing with her pen. "Have something before you leave, Paul."

He attempted to resist this siren's song, but his mother ordered, "Sit and eat, Paul." He did, but only after defiantly getting out a paper plate.

He gulped down leftovers, eschewing the proffered beer, while listening to his mother blithely trot out painful family memories as if every mother depended on charity to feed and clothe her children and every father beat a child who spoke out of turn.

For one thing and one thing alone the Arrendondo children respected him: his iron-fisted insistence on education equipped them to escape the tyranny of their poverty. One by one, they graduated high school, went to college on scholarships and grants, and made a place for themselves far from their old neighborhood, and their parents. When Juanita dismissed her daughters' pleas for her to leave that place, their communication died away. Only Paul continued to go back.

He stood from the table to shove the empty paper plate into the trash can. "Thank you, Jeannine," he said with finality. He bent to kiss his mother's cheek. "I'll call," he promised, glancing at his mother's hostess with the expectation that she would translate all such messages.

"Don't worry about a thing, Paul," Jeannine nodded, and Juanita reached up to pat his back.

He paused by the door to take up his suitcase on the way out. "He's a good boy," Juanita said. "Papa was always proudest of him."

With his head practically hanging out the window, Paul drove to the first car wash he could find in San Angelo. Pulling into the bay, he opened both doors of the cab, plunked in quarters, and turned the power hose on the bench seat. Standing in the driver's side door, he made reasonable efforts to keep the water off the driver's seat while blasting the drainage through the open passenger door. That done, he climbed in for the four-hour drive to Fort Worth with windows cranked all the way down.

It was after two o'clock in the morning when he pulled into the parking lot of the first decent motel he could find on the outskirts of the city limits. He lugged his bags in and pulled out his overworked credit card for the night's lodging. Then he dragged himself to the room, pulled off his boots, and sank back on a wooden mattress and stiff foam pillow.

He awoke the next morning with barely enough time to shave before check-out time at 11:00. (In the city, he was sensitive about maintaining a groomed appearance, as it helped ameliorate first-glance judgments.)

With fresh charges on his card, he went out to his truck to think about what to do next. The seat was still damp; the stain faded but visible; the odor only faintly repellent. First thing, he started up the truck and located a fast-food drive-through next to a mall. Given that the temperature was over one hundred today already, he took his breakfast of biscuits and coffee inside the mall to eat.

Given the vast number of cars crowding the parking lots, he should have awakened earlier to his error, but he did not remember that today was Saturday—the last Saturday before area schools opened—until he entered the coolness of the mall atrium to be assaulted by thousands of kids in full control of mall facilities. Paul gazed briefly at the deafening mob surging through every visible walkway, then he made a sharp about-face to escape outside.

In the wasteland of concrete, there was a little oasis of green grass superintended by three pin oaks. The stone bench underneath them was presently empty, so Paul took his coffee and biscuits over there. He brushed aside cigarette butts and sat heavily to pry off the top of the coffee cup and flip it aside.

"Don't litter." Paul looked up so quickly at the unexpected admonition that he spilled a little coffee on his leg. He then regarded a previously unnoticed companion leaning on one of the oaks, sipping a soft drink. Despite the heat, he also wore jeans, boots, and a long-sleeved cowboy shirt. He looked so much like he had come straight off a ranch himself that Paul bit back an irritated rejoinder about minding one's own business. Peeved, he picked up the plastic top and dropped in the food sack. Then he withdrew a biscuit, unwrapped it, and began eating.

The stranger sipped his drink quietly for a minute before observing, "A little bitter, are we?"

"What?" Paul looked up in astonishment.

"That biscuit is either a personal enemy, or you're really angry about something."

"Do you—would you mind psychoanalyzing some-body else?" Paul sputtered.

"Nah, I like you," the guy said with a vague smile.

Shaking his head, Paul accepted the fact that he was sharing quiet space with a loony, so he gulped breakfast to leave as soon as possible. Wadding up the trash, he stood, looking around for a receptacle, but didn't see one. "I'll take it," the stranger said, extending his hand for the ball of waste paper.

Paul stared at him—mid-thirties, he guessed, with straight dark hair and a hint of Polynesian in his features. But, as invited, Paul handed over the trash and started walking away. "You throwing away money now?" the guy said.

Paul looked back with a retort on his lips when he saw the man bemusedly pulling crumpled bills from the wad of trash. Paul hurried over to him. "What—?"

He slapped his pocketed wallet, where he should still have the two hundred dollars he had withdrawn from the ATM. "Are you—?" He watched, dumbfounded, as the stranger dislodged four wrinkled twenties and handed them to him one at a time.

"I—" Paul accepted the bills, dumbly wondering how he could have gotten cash mixed up in his food order. Or was it from the drive-through cashier? No, the change from the $3 order he had simply tossed into a cup holder.

Finally, he took the wadded sack and opened it up to look in it. Nothing but trash. "I—" He looked into the stranger's quizzical, humorous brown eyes. "Thank you." Without removing his wallet, Paul stuffed the bills in the same back pocket.

The other regarded him with a little sigh of exasperation. "How were you cheated, that you're so bitter?"

Paul threw up his hands. "My father died yesterday, and I spent four thousand dollars that I don't have because my mother didn't want to let him die!"

"So you spent four thousand dollars to give your mother peace of mind that everything that could have been done for your dying father was done. No guilt, no recriminations, just a simple fulfillment of filial duty. Sounds like money well spent to me," the other observed.

Paul stared at him, then dropped his head, muttering, "I know. But . . . I quit my job, and my wife left me. . . ."

A few seconds after he had trailed off into silence, his companion said, "Maybe she felt cheated."

Paul's eyes shot up. "What?"

"She was never supposed to be a maid. She went down there with clearly defined duties that suddenly changed to just doing housework, but maybe you weren't willing to take her side of it—except to tell her to 'get a job in a dress shop,'" he said scornfully.

Paul's hands went clammy. "Who are you?"

"My name is Fletcher Streiker," the other said, watching him.

"You—!" The reclusive billionaire philanthropist. "You were—" Who had been subsidizing Paul's work at the drug treatment center before that last trip to Big Bend. Paul had never met him before, nor even communicated directly with him. Besides the periodic news reports, all Paul knew of him was that it was his name on the checks that kept the center afloat in those early months of Paul's employment at the center. "You pulled funding out from under us without a word!"

"Once you decided to go into business robbing drug runners," Fletcher said coldly. Paul gaped at him. Fletcher went on, "Because you won't take my word for it that I would support you, and you start with these asinine robberies, why should I then invite DEA scrutiny of *my* affairs?

"You created a real breach of trust between Buddy and his parents. You enticed Perry into activity that landed him in jail. And you left a lot of toxic waste by dumping the drugs in Big Bend."

"But—that first year Buddy and I stumbled on the exchange in progress—what else could we do? If Buddy hadn't grabbed the gun, we would have been killed. And then we were left with the drugs that we had to get rid of, and the money—" Paul fell over the words in justifying himself.

"That first encounter was a gift, and the opportunity to provide stopgap assistance until Sheriff Potts could muster the resources to handle the situation." Fletcher said. "You were never given permission to go back for more. But when you did, you thwarted everything he tried to do. And your cute little 'gift' of coke to him very nearly ruined him. I had to remove a good deputy from service after he witnessed the sheriff trying to flush it all." Streiker was distinctly irritated by the inconvenience.

"Oh, God," Paul exhaled. A momentary terror rose up in him that *anybody* would know so much. "I did. It's all true." He slumped down to the bench. Elbows braced on his knees, he held his head. "I knew it was wrong from day one, but I did it anyway." A moment later, he said defensively, "We met Royce and Renetta doing that. We rescued them."

In a devastatingly quiet voice, Fletcher replied, "Once you went out to Big Bend again, and once you had found them, had you not followed your conscience and done your utmost to get them to safety, I guarantee that you're the one who'd be sitting in jail right now, and I'd let you. You did nothing heroic."

"I know," Paul mouthed in surrender. "I know. But . . . I don't know what to do about it now. I don't know how to make things right with Royce. I don't have any idea where she is, even. New York City is a big place."

Fletcher was silent a while, as if deliberating. "She's not in New York. She's here in Fort Worth."

Paul lurched to a stand. "She is! Why? Where?"

Fletcher evaluated him. "It troubles me that the first thing you asked was not, 'Is she all right?'"

Tears sprang to Paul's eyes. Helplessly, he said, "I assumed that if you knew where she was, then she was all right."

"I will accept that," Fletcher said.

A few seconds passed in silence. "Are you going to tell me where she is?" Paul asked meekly.

"If I did, what would you do about it?" Fletcher asked.

Paul exhaled, gesturing, "Try to make it up to her!"

Fletcher weighed that. "Okay," he said, and started to walk off.

"Wait!" Paul sprang after him. "Are you going to help me? Mr. Streiker, I'm begging you to help me find her!"

"Paul," Fletcher said, turning, "let me tell you a great truth: everybody gets what they truly want—not what they *think* they want, but what they genuinely desire in the depths of their heart. Ultimately, this is what they receive."

Paul grappled with this. "Are you telling me that if I truly want her, I'll find her?"

"Yes," Fletcher said.

"But—why won't you just tell me? Or give me a clue to go on?" Paul said, growing angry.

"And deprive you of discovering what you really want? That would be counterproductive, wouldn't it?" Fletcher said mildly.

Paul exhaled, wiping tears from his face. "I . . . I only have two charge cards, and they're about maxed out. I don't see how I can afford to search. . . ."

"Well, I guess that means you can look for her as long as your cash holds out," Fletcher said.

Paul dropped his head in disappointment and Fletcher started to walk off again. "Wait!" Paul cried. "Mr. Streiker, help me!"

Now twenty feet away, Fletcher glanced back. "I did." Then he was gone in the blazing sunlight.

Paul dropped to the hard bench, choking back anger. Sweat dripped down his face to mingle with bitter tears over his failings—and before he had failed Royce, he had failed Streiker.

In hindsight, it was crystal-clear that he'd had numerous opportunities to contact Streiker while he was director of the drug treatment center. If Paul had been more upfront with him then, Streiker never would have revoked funding in the first place. Paul knew better than to even ask him if it was okay to rob the drug runners; he knew what Streiker's answer would have been. Even then, when the checks stopped, Paul had been given a number to call. He just never did.

Suddenly he remembered the feed store in San Angelo—somebody there, of all places, mentioned that they'd gotten a call from this Dallas billionaire who was looking for a particular brand of HDF pellets for a friend's horses.

"Who was that? Garner. That was ol' Russ Garner," Paul muttered. *"Got his number right here,"* Garner had bragged, waving a piece of paper. *"The private number of a Mr. Fletcher Streiker."* And that was hours after Paul's first bad fight with Royce. He remembered feeling the urge to snatch at that paper, but after the funding debacle, he wouldn't consider it. Yet now it appeared that the coincidence of hearing that in the feed store had been an engraved invitation to call. *"Ain't never heard of a Fletcher Streiker,"* somebody else had scoffed, and Garner was left to defend his credibility alone while Paul walked out of the store to a deteriorating situation at home.

What if he had accepted the invitation and called Streiker that day? Since Streiker obviously knew something about the situation at the Ferrings', surely he could have provided some workable alternative for Royce. Was it pride again, preventing him from admitting that he screwed up? Or was it that he simply couldn't believe a billionaire would know or care anything about Paul's personal problems? Whatever it was, it sealed his fate: he had lost Royce, and Streiker had walked off without. . . .

At this point Paul stilled and raised his face. *He said, "I did." What did he mean by that? Past tense; he already helped me. How?*

Thinking hard, he wiped his wet face on his sleeve. Then he reached into his back pocket to extract the crumpled bills as well as his wallet. He opened the wallet to count the cash: two hundred dollars, all still there. Then he smoothed out the four bills to place them in his wallet.

He just gave me eighty dollars so smoothly I never even knew it. It didn't make up for the five thousand he had just spent on his father, but—payment for that was not urgent. Eighty dollars was apparently all he needed right now, in addition to what he had. (The $200 residue in his checking account needed to stay there to cover withdrawals that weren't posted yet.) So how far could he search on $280? That wouldn't even buy a plane ticket to—

He said she's here in Fort Worth, Paul remembered. *She's still here in my hometown, my stomping grounds, so I didn't need money for airfare to anywhere. Where to look? Where to even start?*

Paul floundered a little in the irrationality of it all—that he could find Royce simply if he wanted to badly enough. Then again . . . Streiker was a busy man. Why would he bother giving Paul even this much help unless he knew it wasn't wasted effort?

The thought crossed his mind that Streiker meant what he said: he liked Paul. Despite his screw-ups, Streiker hadn't given up on him.

Paul got up from the bench, put on his sunglasses, and started toward his truck, parked a great distance away. A sudden impulse checked his steps; he hurried back to retrieve the ball of trash and carry it with him till he passed a trash receptacle in the parking lot. It was a trivial obedience, but somehow important.

Thus encouraged, he pulled out his keys and resumed a purposeful stride to his vehicle.

4

Paul sat in his truck, turned the ignition, and backed out of the mall parking space. "Okay." He took a breath, then headed out of the parking lot toward the highway. "I have no idea what I'm doing. Royce has had a month to get acquainted with Fort Worth, so I've got no idea where she might have wound up."

Could he guess where she might have started? Besides the airport, what places did she know here? He braked at a stop sign, looking ahead to the traffic light at the intersection of the freeway. By the time he reached that intersection, he had made up his mind, and turned the wheel toward the Phoenix Street Center downtown.

This was the drug treatment center, and Royce knew where it was. He had taken her there after she had flown down from New York at his invitation. DEA agents were waiting for him, however, and took both him and Royce to their field headquarters just a few blocks away. While interrogating him, they had turned her out onto the street. Somehow, Royce had managed to swipe his keys, get back to the center, find his apartment address, and drive there in the center's Nissan.

He smiled upon remembering how, while thinking she was wandering around Fort Worth, he had stumbled upon her the next morning sleeping in his bed. In his underwear. If he hadn't been due imminently at the airport. . . . Anyway, he had to assume that she was still just as capable of getting around. He couldn't imagine why she would go to the center, but since that was the only place he knew of to start, then start there he would.

He turned onto Phoenix Street and drove slowly past the center's storefront, craning his neck to see what he might. The Nissan was in the fenced lot, and he detected someone standing in the front office. So Paul went on down the street, U-turned, and pulled up to the curb in front of the faded red-brick building. He climbed down from the cab, wiping his mouth. *What am I supposed to say? "Have you seen my runaway wife?"*

As he entered, a man settling behind the front desk looked up. Paul appraised him instantly as a counselor rather than a recovering addict, and approached with extended hand: "Hi, I'm Paul Arrendondo. I used to be director here until about a year ago."

The fellow stood to shake his hand. "Yeah, Arrendondo! The DEA guide at Big Bend! Oh, yeah, I heard all about it. Mitch Grooms. The new director."

"Thank God they found somebody normal," Paul blurted.

Mitch laughed, "Theoretically. What can I do for you?"

"Well—" Paul licked his lips nervously. "My wife Royce might have come by, oh, a month ago, and—"

"Pretty girl, long brown hair?" Mitch asked.

"Yes," Paul said, heart thumping.

"Yeah, I remember her." Mitch sat back down to begin rummaging in the top desk drawer. "She never came back for—here it is. I thought she was going to come back for it, but she never did." He extended a slightly wrinkled sheet of paper.

"Oh?" Paul said. He tried to hold the paper still so he could look at it. "I'm sorry—this is—?"

"Well, she asked for a list of our affiliate treatment centers, and said she'd drop back by to pick it up. She seemed in kind of a hurry. But, after she left, Brad—he was in the other room when we were talking—said he thought what she'd wanted was the address of the parent organization, which is Gold Cord, Incorporated. So I said I'd compile a list of affiliates just in case, and we'd clarify that whenever she came back. Is that what you needed?" Mitch nodded at the paper Paul held.

He raised his brows. "Sure, I think this'll do fine."

"You looking for another director position?" Mitch asked in friendly interest.

"Well, not really. We were kind of discussing that. But Royce wanted to move back to the city, so I'm willing to consider anything." Paul stopped just short of asking Mitch to call him if she came back in. "Anyway, thanks a lot. Good luck with the center."

"Drop back by anytime," Mitch said. They shook hands again and Paul went on out to his truck. He pulled away from the curb, but drove only as far as the nearest public parking in order to stop and process whatever it was he had just learned.

First: how was she getting around? He briefly considered going back to ask Mitch what she was driving, but that might raise more questions than it was worth. She might not be driving anything—a native New York like Royce was used to public transportation. She never drove in San Angelo; she rode with anyone else going into town—usually Jeannine—and, as far as he knew, Royce had never gotten a Texas driver's license.

"Okay," he murmured. Given that tracing her transportation was probably not an option, how could he use the information in front of him—information that she had asked for? He looked over the list: six treatment centers scattered over the Dallas/Fort Worth metroplex. Driving to each would burn up a lot of gas and time. And what was he supposed to say once he got there? But, if he called. . . .

He pulled out his phone and studied it, then dropped it back into his shirt pocket. He put the truck into gear and began coasting through the parking lot, looking for a public phone. They were pretty rare nowadays, but that's where he needed to call from. He didn't want anyone to be able to trace his calls, because . . . he wasn't sure if what he was doing was considered stalking. The last thing he needed now was an arrest.

After fifteen minutes of driving around, he finally located a pay phone outside a convenience store. He went inside to buy a calling card, because some of the calls would be long distance. In doing so, he discovered that his MasterCard was over the limit, as it was rejected. He kept back his American Express (however little available credit was left on it) for emergencies, and paid cash for the calling card, which he took back out to the phone.

Fortunately, it was presently shaded by the building, else the heat radiating off the sidewalk might have made it too uncomfortable to stand here and place any calls. And nobody else was waiting to use the phone.

Sweating, Paul keyed in the card information and dialed the first center—even on a Saturday, someone should answer. "Arapaho Street Center."

"Um, yes," Paul cleared his throat. "Is Royce Arrendondo there, please?"

"Sorry, you have the wrong number." Click.

Taking that at face value, Paul hung up and rekeyed the card numbers to dial center number two. When that call was answered, he asked, "May I speak to Royce Arrendondo?"

"Who?"

"Royce Arrendondo," he repeated.

"I'm sorry—I don't know the name. Is he a counselor or a client?"

"She. I thought she was working there. Maybe I got the wrong clinic. Is this the Beltline Center?" Paul asked, looking at his list.

"Yes. Hold on."

Waiting, Paul swallowed, closing his eyes against the glare from the parking lot. A moment later the center employee came back on the line: "I'm sorry, we don't seem to have her on our list."

"Okay, my mistake. Thanks." He hung up and went back inside the store to get a soft drink. The clerk started upon his entrance and eyed him tensely throughout the twenty-second transaction of cash for a drink.

When he came back out to the pay phone, he sucked on the soft drink for a minute, trying to think if there was a better way to elicit the information he needed without lying. Besides the fact that he was rigidly honest, he knew that lying had a way of boomeranging to knock you on your rear. But no—he couldn't see anything to do other than call and ask for her.

As he set the soft drink atop the phone, a police cruiser pulled up. Paul froze with a hand on the receiver, watching the lone officer get out and approach him. "*Ola*, pal. Let's see an ID."

Gritting his teeth, Paul hung up and brought out his wallet with his driver's license. The cop looked it over, asking, "What are you doing?"

"I'm . . . placing a call," Paul answered.

"Who to?" the cop asked. He surveyed Paul's clothing without touching him, evidently looking for a weapon.

Immediately, Paul guessed that his own behavior looked suspicious to the clerk inside—it probably appeared that he was either casing the place to rob it, or making drug sales over the phone. (Little did he guess that the clerk actually suspected him of terrorist activities.)

So Paul showed the cop the list Mitch had given him. "I believe a friend of mine is at one of these drug treatment centers. I'm trying to find her." And he hoped that the cell phone in his shirt pocket was not visible.

The officer looked over the sheet, then gestured to his truck. "Can I search your vehicle there?"

"Yes," Paul said tightly, watching the cop casually wave his driver's license around. He waited by the phone while the officer went through his toolbox in the bed of the truck, then the cab, which fortunately smelled so bad, he didn't spend long in there. But he did unload the luggage to look through it. Paul kept quiet, determined not to further delay his own search by losing his temper.

Finding nothing suspicious in Paul's possessions, the cop sat in his cruiser with Paul's driver's license to type at his onboard computer, all the while keeping an eye on him. Leaning against the wall by the phone, Paul watched him as well, knowing that he was checking for outstanding warrants. As long as Paul kept his cool, the officer should just leave him be. Paul had already demonstrated that he was not simply loitering.

Shortly, the cop came back to hand him his driver's license. "Okay, how much longer you going to be?"

"Look, it's a public phone, and I don't see anybody waiting," Paul protested. At the other's hard look, he amended, "Just a few more minutes."

"Okay," the cop said. Paul watched while he went in to talk to the clerk, then come out to his car and leave.

Paul debated leaving too, but as he might encounter the same questions at another phone, he decided to finish what he was doing here. With that, he called center number three. He may have been a little brusque asking, "May I speak to Royce Arrendondo?"

"Who's calling?" replied a woman's voice.

Paul paused only an instant. "This is her husband, Paul."

"I'm sorry; we don't give out any information over the telephone." And the woman hung up.

Slowly, he depressed the switchhook, thinking. That could mean she had been there, or not. Was there any way to rule out the possibility? He redialed the number. When the same woman answered, he said quietly, "This is Paul again. All I want to know is that my wife got the help she needed. She was in a real bad way when she left —you don't have to tell me where she is; I just want to know that she got help."

The woman paused. "What was the name again?"

"Royce Arrendondo."

"Hold on a moment."

She put him on hold and he waited, taking a long drink. Then she came back on the line and said, "I'm sorry; she hasn't been here."

"Thank you; I'll check elsewhere."

"Good luck," she said sincerely, and he hung up.

Crossing number three off his list, he went on to number four: "Hello, is Royce Arrendondo there?"

"Hold on; let me check," the male voice said, and Paul's throat constricted. He waited with the handset pressed so hard against his ear that it hurt. Was she actually working there? Would she come to the phone? Finally, the male came back on the line: "Uh, I don't see her name on the schedule. When did she start?"

"Should've been about three weeks ago," Paul blustered. "But I can't remember whether she said—" he glanced down at his list—"the Bowie Street Center or the Beltline Center."

"Oh," the guy said, enlightened. "Must have been the Beltline Center, 'cause I don't see the name any-where."

"My mistake. Sorry," Paul said.

"No problem."

On to center number five. Paul took a long draw on the soft drink, keyed in the calling-card numbers, and dialed. No answer, except for a machine. Not about to leave a message, he bypassed that one for now and went on to center number six—the last one. He dialed and waited, feeling his stomach knot up.

"Preston Road Center."

"Yes, may I speak to Royce Arrendondo, please?"

The man on the other end paused. "Who's calling, please?"

"This is her husband, Paul."

"And . . . what makes you think your wife is here?"

"I thought she was working there," Paul explained.

"Not to my knowledge," the man said firmly.

"I'm sorry; I must have the wrong number," Paul said.

"I guess so."

And that was that—except for center number five. Paul called that number again; hearing the answering machine again, he hung up, wiping sweat from his face with his sleeve. *This is futile*, he thought, staring down at the wrinkled sheet. *This is not going to get me any closer to finding Royce*. Of course, once he found her—and found that she was okay—then convincing her to come back (where?) with him was a whole 'nother proposition.

"It's a total waste of time," he muttered. He looked again at the address for center number five: Grauwyler Road Center. "That's way out in Irving," he noted, displeased. But, actually, it wasn't that far. And considering that his calendar seemed pretty well open for the rest of the day, he climbed back into his truck, turned on the air conditioner with relief, and headed east.

He wound his way through Saturday traffic to Grauwyler Road, swerving slightly here and there to read street numbers along the way. Then he abruptly turned into a stripfront shopping center and cruised through the front parking lots until he came to the space that had "Grauwyler Road Center" printed in large black letters on its front window. Paul had parked and approached the storefront's door before seeing the other sign: "Closed Until Further Notice."

Hands on hips, he dropped his head. That was it, then. There was no place else to check. Returning to his truck, he threw himself onto the seat, flipping the air conditioner to *high* while he crumpled the sheet and tossed it out the window. Then he raised the window and sat steaming.

It suddenly occurred to him: what if she had changed her name back to Lindel? What if Royce Lindel, not Royce Arrendondo, had gone to any one of centers 1 through 6? He couldn't very well go back and ask now. It was hopeless.

Why wouldn't Streiker just tell him where she was, if he expected him to find her? Was Streiker just jerking him around? Like he jerked the funding out from under him? Like he—

Paul reseated his sunglasses guiltily, aborting that line of thought. It wasn't right, and it wasn't productive. He understood perfectly well why Streiker had done it; understood so well that even the explanation was unnecessary. So if Streiker held out hope that Paul could find her with the information he'd already been given, Paul had to assume that Streiker's faith in him was genuine.

Reluctantly, he set himself to mentally retrace his steps in order to ascertain what he knew. Actually—he knew a lot. Royce *had* been to the Phoenix Street

Center; she had gone there seeking information. And she hadn't been back. Why?

The most obvious answer was that she had found the information she was looking for elsewhere. Mitch had prepared a list of all the centers; Paul had checked each one of those and found nothing, apparently. So that wasn't the information she wanted. But Brad thought that she had been asking about the parent company—

Paul climbed out of his truck to retrieve the wadded-up sheet. He sat behind the wheel again and smoothed the sheet on his leg. The last address and phone number were for that parent company: Gold Cord, Inc.

He flipped out his phone to dial the number. He was not surprised at all, late Saturday afternoon, to hear a recorded message thanking him for his call and begging him to call back during normal office hours. Noting the Dallas address, Paul fastened his seat belt and turned the wheel. Then he paused: Streiker had said she was in Fort Worth, not Dallas. Paul would be straying out of his parameters to look that far away from Fort Worth.

He shook his head, progressing out of the parking lot onto Grauwyler. If the company had offices all over the metroplex, and she was at one of those, then checking headquarters was still the most viable means of finding her. He doubted anyone would be there now, but he still wanted to see the building and make sure there was no "out of business" sign on the door. If it was close to downtown (as he assumed) it should take him less than an hour to get there.

Blending with traffic going east on the freeway, he wondered whether he shouldn't go to the police with a missing person complaint, after all. They'd ask a lot of uncomfortable questions about why she left, but, with her Social Security number and birth date, they'd surely be able to find an address—

A home address. He suddenly realized that he was concentrating exclusively on finding where she worked, not where she lived. Was if she was living with someone? His truck swerved slightly at the involuntary tightening of his hand. Is that why Streiker hesitated before even telling him that she was in Fort Worth, population half a million?

It was such a daunting question that he had to exit the freeway to stop and think. The first available place to stop was a gas station, so he pulled in to fill the tank while assessing this new complication. Is that why she wouldn't return his phone calls? Because she'd found someone else? Then why should he even try to find her? She knew his phone number; let her call him!

Replacing the gas pump nozzle, Paul shook his head. "You're jumping to conclusions. Assuming something you don't know"—and justifying himself at her expense.

Dimly, he began to perceive the wisdom behind Streiker's reticence. If Paul wasn't sure that he wanted Royce back *regardless*, it was pointless—even detrimental—for Streiker to tell him where she was. It was easy enough for Paul to *say* he wanted to find her, but Streiker, and Paul himself, needed to see if Paul was willing to back up his words with time and effort.

If that was the case, then (and this was a new thought) if Paul persevered and came to a hopeless dead end, Streiker might step in with something a little more helpful. Encouraged by this thought, Paul proceeded toward Dallas, and the headquarters of Gold Cord.

Shortly after arriving in downtown Dallas, Paul realized that, in fact, he had no idea where Gold Cord was. So, heroically, he stopped at a gas station to ask directions. The clerk (a lot less suspicious than the convenience store clerk) pulled up an online map to help him find it. Contrary to expectation, it was not one of the modern, gleaming buildings that dominated downtown —it was a house, actually, in the historic district (such as it was, dating from the early 1900s) all of five minutes from the gas station.

Rechecking the address on the thoroughly wrinkled sheet, Paul passed the house twice before pulling up to the curb in front of it. He climbed down from the cab and went up the front walk, wondering what he would say if the residents answered the door in their Saturday casuals. Did he inquire for "Royce Arrendondo" or "Royce Lindel"? That kind of detail he really needed to work out before he talked to anyone here, assuming this address had anything to do with his search.

Only when he reached the front door and took off his sunglasses did he spot the discreet bronze plaque announcing, "Gold Cord, Inc." Thus emboldened, he rang the doorbell and stepped back to look at the side windows for signs of movement. Nothing happened in response. Not surprised, he backed up toward the steps, but waited just a moment more, just in case someone might have to come downstairs to answer the door.

It suddenly opened, and he stared at the cleaning lady who laid aside a dust mop to look at him inquiringly. "My name is Paul Arrendondo," he blurted. "Mr. Streiker sent me here to find my wife, Royce." Wait—was that anywhere near true?

She withdrew from the doorway, jerking her head over her shoulder. "No one's here, but you can come have a look. I'm almost done, though," she warned him.

"Thank you. I won't be but a moment," he said, entering. As he tucked his sunglasses in his shirt pocket, his eyes swept a beautiful old sitting room decorated in rose and deep green.

"The office is back there," she said, gesturing, and took up the dust mop again.

"Thank you," Paul repeated. Sweat sprang out on his face when he crossed the threshold into the small room, glancing over the two desks, computers, and filing cabinets.

Where to start? The unexpected opportunity almost paralyzed him. He looked at a computer, then rejected attempting to circumvent passwords or breach legitimate security. He didn't even know what kind of a business this was, or what confidential records they might keep.

Seeing a large card file beside a telephone, he leaned over to flip through it. Mostly business contacts, he deduced. Now, if Royce was a client or employee, where would her records be?

He turned to the four-drawer filing cabinet standing next to the desk. With sweaty palms, he tugged on the top drawer, and it opened. Thumbing through the files, he saw they were indexed by names, which appeared to be alphabetized. He was in the "A's." Flipping through the files—"Aaron, Michael," "Abrams, Celeste," "Amhurst, Patrice,"—he froze over a slender file labeled, "Arrendondo, Royce."

5

Paul pulled Royce's file out of the drawer with shaking hands and opened it up. There was a single sheet with brief handwritten notes. He started to just take the sheet, but, remembering by whose name he had gained entrance, he decided against theft of confidential records. So he opened the desk copier and ran the sheet through it. By the time he had replaced the original in the filing cabinet, the cleaning lady appeared in the doorway. "You about done?"

"Yes. Thank you," he said, folding the copy. He preceded her to the front door, adding, "Have a nice weekend."

"Yeah, you too," she returned. He stepped onto the porch and she closed the door behind him. He listened to the deadbolt slide into place, then trotted down the front walk to his truck.

He was so distracted that he almost pulled away from the curb in front of a passing car. A long blare of the other driver's horn recalled him to the immediate necessity of getting to someplace quiet so that he could calm down and assess what he had found. He discovered that he was hungry, too; since the Saturday-night feeding frenzy in Dallas had not yet commenced, he soon located a nice little diner that was still relatively quiet. Securing a corner table, he ordered a number 6 and a beer on tap. When his beer arrived, he took a swig, unfolded the copy, and spread it out to study it.

It was an interview form with some of the blanks partially filled in by hand. At the top, it was dated July 18 of this year—days after Royce had left the ranch, as far as he could remember. (Here he winced: How callous was it that he wasn't sure of the exact date she had left?) Also at the top was "M. Davis"—obviously, the name of the counselor or interviewer. Beneath the name was some kind of identification number.

The handwritten notes continued with Royce's name (spelled correctly) and a phone number which he recognized as her cell phone that had been disconnected. Next was "San Angelo, Grayson-Faring"—where she had come from, misspelled.

The waitress appeared with Paul's dinner of chipped beef; he moved the sheet to make room for the plate. After taking a few bites and another sip of beer, he returned to the notes. In a block headed "Explanation" was first written: "no work no money"—Was that a complaint of the situation at the ranch or an assessment of her circumstances as of July 18? "husband unresponsive"—Paul wilted, taking another sip. "no abuse"

"There certainly wasn't," he muttered vehemently. Which, in a way, made it worse: Royce had not been overdramatizing the situation. So when she said he was "unresponsive," that was not an exaggeration, either.

"another woman" "What?" gasped Paul. "wife second on list" He stared at the words over his cooling dinner.

She must have been talking about Jeannine. In their last argument, one of Royce's complaints had to do with the amount of attention he bestowed on the presiding woman of the house: *"Whatever she wants comes first!"*

This he had dismissed with something about Jeannine being their employer. Royce had followed that up with the observation that it shouldn't mean he was on call 24 hours a day, 7 days a week. *"We never have any alone time,"* she said. *"We never go anywhere, just you and me."*

Paul lifted his eyes to the neon lights outside in the twilight. That was a valid complaint; why couldn't he address it? What had he told her? He couldn't remember. Probably nothing but an excuse. He did remember her next request: *"Let's get a place of our own in San Angelo."* That a gal from New York City should be reduced to begging for a place in comparatively tiny San Angelo was significant to the point of writing across the sky.

And what had he said to *that?* Again, he couldn't remember. (Point to ponder: why was remembering what she had said so much easier than remembering what he had said? Because she made too much sense for him to come up with a decent rebuttal?) He did remember that he had ultimately rejected the idea without further discussion because it would be "inconvenient." And she had said nothing more before leaving a day or two later.

Paul laid the notes aside to finish his dinner. The little café had filled up around him with an exponential increase in noise—dishes clattering, phones chirping, children wailing—He flagged down the waitress to get his check, which he paid in cash, with a five-dollar tip. Then he went out to his truck to seek a quieter place to finish the self-torture of reading these notes.

He cruised past restaurants, coffee shops, and stores looking for someplace lighted and reasonably quiet, but the sheer number of vehicles spilling out of parking lots on either hand did not look promising. "Shee, doesn't anybody stay home on Saturday night?" he muttered.

Yes. He did. Those last few weeks—deep down, he sensed that something was wrong with Walt; the old boy just wasn't able to do the work anymore. So the less Walt did, the more Paul attempted to take up the slack for him. And there was so much, so much that needed to be done, they could've easily taken on two more hands full-time.

So by the time Saturday night rolled around, all he wanted was to crawl into bed. But Royce, after a boring, restless week of keeping house, wanted to *go out*. *"Can't we get away for just a* little while*? Are you indentured here?"* This also fell on deaf ears, because by the time she got that much out, he was sound asleep (or too tired to argue).

Paul happened upon the downtown public library and immediately pulled into the lighted parking lot. He parked and trotted up the stone steps, peering through the glass doors. No one here but homeless men looking at porn on the library computers, as was their constitutional right. Paul chose a conspicuous seat in the wide-open lobby (so the security guard could comfortably keep an eye on him) and spread out the dreaded sheet on the table in front of him.

Bypassing what he had already read, he absorbed the next notation: "needs work right away." Yes, she probably did; so what did they do about it?

Brief, almost illegible phrases noted her work history: "appt. sec'y to Jeanine Faring," "Chocolate Conglomerate (children's book publisher) NYC," "writing, editing, publishing."

There followed a column of numbers—five separate numbers, it appeared. Two—the first and fourth—were crossed out. The other three had check marks beside them. They were all 10-digit numbers. The first checked number had 201 for its first three digits, which he recognized as a New Jersey area code.

Disturbed, Paul took out his phone and dialed that number. Discordant tones followed, with the computerized apology: "I'm sorry; the number you dialed is no longer in service. Please hang up and dial again."

With drawn brows, he tried the second number, which had a 357 area code. (*357? Where is that?*) This produced a blank buzz. For the third number, Paul accessed reverse lookup on his phone and entered the digits. The text message was returned: "invalid area code."

Paul sat back as the realization dawned on him: these weren't phone numbers. They meant something else.

He stared down at the sheet. How in the world could he find out what they meant? Then his eyes were drawn back to the top of the sheet, to the heading: "Client Information," and to the small print in the bottom right-hand corner: "Gold Cord, Inc. Form 86-A, rev. 8-04."

This was a company form. To interpret it, he needed to know more about the company.

Paul raised his eyes to the row of public computers. Abruptly, he got up to sit at a vacant monitor between two other disreputable internet surfers. He called up a search engine and entered "Gold Cord Inc." From the list of results, he clicked on the company's home page and settled down to read.

The website explained that Gold Cord was a private social services company; the name was taken from the title of a book by Amy Carmichael, the Christian missionary to India. In explaining how she came up with the title, Ms. Carmichael wrote in the Foreword, "'What holds you together?' they asked; and we answered, 'A gold cord.'"

"Our vision of the Gold Cord is that of a lifeline of practical assistance to those in need. Rarely does that involve simple handouts, but offering direction, education, and equipping for profitable work and a stable lifestyle," the webpage said.

All well and good. Get specific, Paul thought, clicking on links within the site. There was a staff page, with names, photos, and short bios of the executives of Gold Cord; there was a map page with a photo of the headquarters in the historic district that he'd already visited; there was a page outlining the services provided by the company. This page contained a list of (with maps and directions to) the six drug treatment centers, a birthing and neonatal center, three area preschools, and a food bank.

Paul's eye settled on the list of preschools—she could be working at one of those. Then he reconsidered:

why did he think that? Royce never showed any desire or aptitude for working with children. And if Gold Cord had any kind of effective work-placement program, it must entail contacts to place job-seekers outside of the organization, in their stated fields.

Paul clicked through the whole website again, then sat back in dissatisfaction. There was no listing of specific jobs—nothing that might correspond to the string of numbers on her interview sheet. But they *must* mean something, and there *must* be a way to access it—

He sat up, leaning forward to click back to the home page. And there it was—how could he have missed it?—A log-in. There were blank fields for a log-in name and password.

Paul looked back down at his sheet, at the top, where the counselor had written his name and number—

"All right, gentlemen; closing time. Clear out, now." The security guard came behind the row of researchers, tapping the backs of their chairs. Paul calmly closed the browser and stood, pushing in the chair. At least he knew what to do next—but he still needed a computer and was unwilling to wait until the library opened again tomorrow afternoon.

He trotted down the library steps and strode across the parking lot to his truck. Sitting behind the wheel, he started the engine and turned on the headlights. Then he sat thinking. Where to find a computer with internet connection on a Saturday night?

For the next forty minutes, he drove around, looking. Not finding anything open but party places downtown, he took the freeway north, to the suburbs. He cruised in heavy traffic, keeping an eye on the array of restaurants and shopping centers on either side of the freeway.

Spotting a promising venue on the southbound frontage road, he U-turned at the first available underpass to cruise south until he could pull into the crowded parking lot of a huge entertainment arcade. He had to drive around another ten minutes to find a parking place, and spent another five minutes walking to the front entrance. But as soon as he entered the lobby to be engulfed by lights and noise, he knew he'd find what he needed here.

He bypassed the bowling alley and pool tables, merely glancing back to the motion theater, dance machine, and laser tag room. The video arcades he also passed by, coming to a room of internet gamers. Here, he showed his driver's license and was given a release to sign affirming that he was over 14 years of age.

The same release warned him that expectations of privacy on the arcade's computers were illusory; should he access illegal or pornographic material, or disseminate same, he could certainly expect a visit from the appropriate authorities. This Paul signed with barely a quiver of conscience, without considering how illegal it might be to impersonate a Gold Cord counselor.

Next, he was allowed to purchase a $40 card good for two hours of computer time. Parting with that much of his cash hurt, but time could only be bought in hour increments, and he didn't want the computer to shut down while he was in the middle of a crucial search.

Then he had to wait for a computer to become available—Saturday night, you know, the place was packed. He was on the tail end of a line of four people. Restless, he looked into the computer room, where nobody seemed ready to leave. "Hey, uh," Paul motioned to the attendant, "what if the place closes before I get on?"

The employee looked at him with an incredulous smirk. "Dude, we're open till two A.M. You'll get on."

"Oh. Right," Paul said.

A twenty-something guy rushed up to the line. He zeroed in on Paul: "Hey! We need a fourth for laser tag! Come on! Your way's paid."

"No, thanks." Paul looked ahead as someone came out and the first person in line gained entrance to the hallowed hall.

"Oh, come *on*—" the guy began pleading.

A small kid who hardly looked 14 glanced back from his place in front of Paul. "I'll play."

"Uh, right." The seeker looked over his head for other volunteers.

But the kid flipped out his wallet to show an ID card. "I'm a certified LaserWorld Terminator."

"Then come on!" The laser-tag player hauled him away, which left Paul another step closer to the computer room. Within fifteen minutes he was shown to a half-stall with a monitor and keyboard. Paul plopped onto the stool, swiped the card through the reader, and watched the internet browser open up on the monitor. *Okay, I'm connected.*

Relocating the joystick back out of the way, he spread the creased form beside the keyboard and brought up the Gold Cord website. On the website's log-in, he entered "M. Davis" and the six-digit number from the form. The page reappeared with the red warning, "Login failed. Invalid name or password."

He tried again, entering, "MDavis" and the number. The warning was repeated: "Login failed. Invalid name or password."

Paul wiped his mouth and tried a third time, typing, "mdavis" with the same number. To his gratification, this opened up a menu page.

He leaned forward to study the selections: "Activity Log," "Employee Handbook," "Insurance Forms," "Company Directory," "Recent Memos," etc., etc. He stirred restlessly, looking. Then he saw a linked reference to "Employment Codes." Clicking on that link opened a page with three columns of ten-digit numbers, formatted exactly like those on Royce's sheet.

"Here we go," he murmured. Noting the first number on her sheet, that with the 201 "area code," he scrolled through the columns until he found it. This was also linked; clicking on it brought up an employment application for a Dallas-based magazine.

Whipping out his pen from his pocket, Paul wrote the name and address of the magazine next to its corresponding number on the sheet. With begrudging respect at the efficiency, he noted that the application could be filled out online and uploaded directly to the employment office of the hiring firm.

He went on to locate the next number, but it had no corresponding link—nothing to click on, and no information besides the number itself. He put a question mark beside that one before discovering the small asterisked note at the bottom of the webpage: "Employers lacking hyperlinks have been temporarily withdrawn from the system." Since there was no way to know whether this employer had been active in the system when Royce was looking for a job, he had to skip it for now.

Why did I sit on my hands and wait for so long before starting to look for her? he wondered with a guilty pang. Then he realized that, even were he burning to find her, it wouldn't have done any good as long as the situation at the ranch remained unchanged. Given everything that the Ferrings had done for him—giving him a place to live and a place to work after he had been booted out of the ministry (and before he started working for the clinic)—he felt obligated to stand by Walt to the end, even at the expense of his own wife.

He never intended to pit one obligation against the other; that's just the way it happened. With Walt's death, however, he was freed up to make Royce a priority. Though it was late in coming, the fact that it was the right thing to do spurred him on.

He continued to scroll through columns until he located the third number. This number was linked, and clicking on it brought up an employment application for . . . The Streiker Corporation.

Paul sat chewing on this for a long time. Is that how Streiker knew where she was—because he'd given her a job? Is that why he wasn't all that anxious for Paul to find her? Grimly, he wrote down the corporate phone number, but didn't bother with the address. The company was international. They had offices every-where. She could be anywhere.

He said she was in Fort Worth, Paul reminded himself. Was she really?

He leaned back so suddenly on the backless stool that he almost lost his balance. How many thousands of employees did Streiker have? So was it not just a little unreasonable (paranoid, even) for Paul to think Streiker was hiding Royce while taunting Paul with the possibility of finding her?

How did he *know where to find* me? Paul suddenly wondered. And it dawned on him that meeting Streiker outside the mall today was not an accident. However he did it, Streiker found him for the explicit purpose of getting him started on his search—even giving him money to start on. So if Paul was going to make any progress at all, he had to accept once for all that whatever Streiker told him was the truth.

Returning to the interview sheet, Paul noted the name of the Dallas-based magazine and ran a search for its website. After he had found it, a few minutes' perusal told him that, while they glanced at events around the metroplex from time to time, the magazine was primarily focused on life in Dallas. If Royce got a job there, she would be living in Dallas, not Fort Worth. So Paul felt reasonably safe ruling out the magazine—which apparently meant that The Streiker Corporation was her new employer.

Since he had computer time left, Paul spent a few minutes on the Streiker site, which, predictably, told him nothing. The corporation was far too large and diverse for more than superficial information to be supplied on a webpage. Meanwhile, running a search on her name within the site produced no results.

Deliberately, Paul swiveled away from the console to lean his elbows on his knees and think. If he went back to Streiker and said, *"My wife is apparently in your employ; would you help me get hold of her* now?*"* what would he say? Did Paul even want to do that? What if he called the Streiker switchboard Monday and asked to talk to her?

Inhaling, Paul sat up to glance at the monitor that still showed the Streiker homepage. At the bottom of the page was a quotation, apparently from the founder himself: "The danger lies in not seeking to make any further progress."

"Uh . . . yeah," Paul muttered. "Thanks for that."

He closed the browser window and stood, drained. As soon as he stepped away from the computer, a teenager darted up. "You done there?"

Paul glanced back at the computer. With no "further progress" to be made till Monday, all he wanted now was a bed. "Yeah. It's all yours."

The boy sat, checked the monitor, then swiveled on the stool. "Hey! You forgot to log out, and you've got, like, thirty minutes left. . . ." But Paul was gone.

The young man struggled over this for a minute. Computer time was expensive, and he could use that guy's log-in to play his game.

But . . . that was dishonest. It was stealing somebody else's minutes. Besides, he wanted to play under his own screen name, so that everybody would know who they got beat by. So the kid saved Paul's minutes for him, logged him off, and logged himself on: "Mighty Theseus."

Meanwhile, Paul had returned to his truck, eyeing the motel across the freeway. After sleeping in rural quiet for a year, he couldn't imagine bedding down with the roar of traffic right outside.

So he climbed into the truck and turned the wheel

onto the freeway, driving north. His destination for tomorrow was west, back to Fort Worth. Motels and hotels were liberally scattered along the main arteries between Dallas and Fort Worth—I-20 and I-30—but there were also smaller highways that boasted a rest stop or two. So he detoured onto the first farm road that intersected the freeway and continued west.

Traffic thinned to the occasional drunk out for a joyride. Apart from the sheer terror of swerving to avoid those weaving headlights, Paul passed the next thirty minutes in quiet travel.

A mom-and-pop motel appeared off the two-lane roadway; Paul immediately exited and pulled up to the front under the neon "vacancy" sign. Two other vehicles, one a pickup and the other an old Suburban, also sat out front.

With a sigh, Paul climbed out of the cab lugging both suitcases. He made sure his toolbox was locked up, then shouldered his way into the vacant lobby. Glancing around, he took his bags to the unmanned front desk. It was past eleven o'clock.

"Hello?" he called, looking toward a glassed-in room off the front desk area. There was movement, and a young woman came listlessly to the desk. "I need a room for one night," he said, pulling out his wallet.

"Single?" she drawled, looking him up and down.

He glanced up. "A single bed, yeah." He paused over his credit cards. The MasterCard was maxed out—that he already knew. The American Express was questionable.

"There's a ten percent discount for cash," she said in a low voice.

"Uh, yeah, okay," he exhaled, flipping through his diminishing stash. "How much?"

"Eighty-five," she murmured, writing something. As Paul began to withdraw the cash, her eyes darted up at someone's imminent approach. "Pay in the morning," she said hurriedly.

"What?" He looked up.

"Pay me in the morning," she whispered. In a louder voice, she said, "That's room one-oh-eight—right around the corner to your left." She held out a key with a plastic tag stamped with the room number.

In some confusion, Paul repocketed his wallet and took the key. "Okay. Thanks." He took up his bags and turned out of the lobby, passing an older gentleman who nodded. Then Paul went out and around the corner till he found the designated room. He let himself in with the key and switched on the light.

It was spartan but reasonably clean—bed, desk, chair, lamp, old but functional toilet, tub and sink. The first thing he did was wedge the chair up under the doorknob, as these old locks could be sprung with a plastic card. Then he showered, stretched out on the bed, and immediately fell asleep.

He awoke early the following morning, grumpy and hungry. Since all he had to do was shave and dress, he was back at the front desk before seven o'clock.

As he half-expected, it was vacant. "Hello?" he called. Dropping his bags in front of the counter, he stepped toward the glassed-in room. "Hello?"

"Yeah." The voice came from behind him, and Paul turned to see the older man he had passed in the lobby last night.

"Yeah. I just need to check out," Paul said, handing him his key while the fellow situated himself behind the counter.

"All right, there. Room one oh eight—" The man paused, peering at an index card, then grinned engagingly over his dentures at Paul. "There'll be no charge, 'Mr. Smith,'" he winked.

6

"Excuse me?" Paul said in astonishment.

"Was your room okay? Find everything to your satisfaction?" the proprietor asked solicitously.

"Well—yes—but I'm not—"

"Then there's no charge, 'Mr. Smith.' We just want to make sure you have a pleasant stay," the gentleman said firmly.

"Oookay," Paul murmured, bending to pick up his bags. "Uh, thanks."

"Don't mention it," the fellow beamed.

Feeling vaguely guilty, Paul tossed his luggage into his truck and departed the motel, driving west. Shortly, he came upon a Denny's, which he pulled up to with relief. Early Sunday morning, the parking lot contained a mere sprinkling of vehicles, but the restaurant was open.

He was immediately seated; almost as quickly he had ordered bacon and eggs, orange juice and coffee. While waiting for his food, he mulled over the weirdness at the motel. He pulled out his wallet, and the thought crossed his mind, *That mix-up saved me eighty-five dollars. Five more than what Streiker gave me.* What was significant about that, of course, was the fact that he could look for Royce as long as his cash held out.

The waitress brought him a glass of orange juice and a carafe of coffee. He poured himself a steaming cup, left it black, and sipped cautiously. *Was it a mix-up?* Last night, the girl at the counter was about to take his money—cash—until the old man started coming over, then she changed her mind and told him to pay in the morning. But, she wasn't there, the old man was, and whatever she had written down made him think—

Paul set down the cup in apprehension: the girl was scamming the old man. She was taking cash when she could, then writing off the patron as somebody important, somebody deserving of a free night—possibly a "mystery guest" who wrote reviews for a travel guide. "Mr. Smith," Paul snorted to himself. He hadn't shown her any identification, nor had she asked, because she had already created an identity for him.

His conscience whispered that he should go back to the motel and tell the old guy what was going on in his establishment. But Paul's common sense, informed by his experience, contravened the suggestion: he was only surmising what had happened; he didn't have all the facts, and it was stupid to aggressively attempt to correct other people's misapprehensions. Let the fellow run his place however he chose—the girl obviously worked there with his knowledge and permission, and the old man knew her better than Paul did. The upshot was: he came away with a free night's stay.

He finished a satisfying breakfast, then rose from the table, leaving cash enough for the check and a two-dollar tip. On the way out, he suddenly stopped short. Returning to the table, he pulled out his wallet and deposited another $5 atop the ones. He just felt that he ought to be generous, after having been given a free night's stay in the motel, and all. . . .

But he still had a day to kill. So he got back into the truck (really weary of the smell) and headed over to Fort Worth. Once within the city limits, he got a soft drink and just drove around aimlessly for a little while. Conscious of wasting gas, he finally pulled into a park beside a pond and got out to sit on a shaded bench.

He sipped his drink, looking out over the dull green water. Restless, he got up to walk around the pond, dislodging clumps of dried mud with the toe of his boot to see what was underneath. Today was Sunday. Before he could stop himself, he was thinking back to a previous existence when Sunday meant getting up at five A.M. to pray and go over his sermon notes.

He kicked mud clods harder by the moment—he couldn't help it; that's why he avoided revisiting that part of his life. He had served that selfish, contrary group of people with all the humility he possessed, but nothing he did was ever enough.

So when his wife Kris left him, they seized on that excuse to examine him under a microscope, find him lacking, and fire him. The clods that went flying from the toe of his boot flung back at him bits of the last sermon he had ever preached, on Job:

> I loathe my very life;
> therefore I will give free rein to my complaint
> and speak out in the bitterness of my soul. . . .

I will say to God:
Does it please you to oppress me,
to spurn the work of your hands? . . .

Do you have eyes of flesh?
Do you see as a mortal sees? . . .
Your hands shaped me and made me.
Will you now turn and destroy me?
Remember that you molded me like clay.
Will you now turn me to dust again? . . .

Why then did you bring me out of the womb?
I wish I had died before any eye saw me.
If only I had never come into being,
or had been carried straight from the womb to the grave!

Are not my few days almost over?
Turn away from me so I can have a moment's joy
before I go to the place of no return,
to the land of gloom and deep shadow.

Ironically, a number of his congregation told him afterwards, with tears in their eyes, that it was the most moving sermon they'd ever heard. With nothing to lose that day, having already been fired, Paul had prepared for it in a manner radically different from his normal routine.

Instead of researching hermeneutics and critical thought, all he did was bare his soul first to God, then to the church. He had seldom experienced such nakedness in prayer before or since, and that sermon was the result.

He told them he was angry and hurt, and he told them why. They ate it up.

But he rebuffed the compliments he received, first, because some of the very people patting him on the back had just voted to fire him, and second, he knew even then that he had ripped the scripture from its context—that wasn't the end of Job's story. The corollary was that it was also not the end of Paul's story, but he did not have the ability to see to the last page. All he could do was live it out one page at a time, and . . . pray for the will to keep going.

He reseated his sunglasses in the brightness of the day. Praying was something he never did very well. When God didn't answer his prayers the way he wanted, he basically gave it up. The only prayers he had seen to be effective (in provoking some kind of response) were those of desperation, as when he knew Royce was wandering in the desert and he couldn't find her. The answer to that prayer came almost immediately: he looked up and saw her lying on the ground. It was a prayer motivated solely and sincerely for her well-being.

So, if he prayed for God to help him find Royce, how much would that be for her well-being? There was no question that she needed him to find her in the desert, but, did she need him to find her now?

Paul dropped his head. He could conjecture all day long, but that question was unanswerable until he did find her. So, almost unwillingly, almost unconsciously, he prayed for help to find her. There was not even the formality of words, as Paul was too distrustful of the catch phrases he had used in past petitions to the Almighty. There was just the desire that rose in him to regain the opportunity to be what she needed.

Another hour passed while he watched ripples created by a frog, or maybe a catfish, disturb the smoothness of the water, and he continued to think. He thought about the ranch, where his life had been pared down to the basics of eating, sleeping, and dealing with stupid animals. This Walt excelled at; he knew exactly how to handle them, knew when they were sick and when they were just contrary. Walt would've been a great pastor.

Paul hung his head, grieving that this life, too, had passed away. He missed Walt—missed him more than Royce. It was a disconcerting revelation, but now he saw that it was true, and why: he trusted Walt in a way that he never quite trusted Royce.

Walt was totally transparent and predictable; he thought in clearly defined lines and used the same phrases over and over again. Once you were in Walt's good graces, nothing you could do (short of murder) would shake his faith in you (and even then, he'd say you were provoked).

Paul never had to prove himself, even when he should have. When Buddy had finally confessed the robberies to his parents, they should have kicked Paul out on his behind the next time he showed up. Instead, Walt had simply said, *"I could really use your help around here full-time. Might keep you out of trouble elsewhere."*

But Royce was a woman, and women were unfathomable. They'd cry, they'd throw fits, they'd create drama, all because you didn't "understand." He always felt as if he was waiting for the other shoe to drop, and it finally did. He loved Royce, no question about it, but they—she—

Paul abruptly stopped where he was, unaware of the mud creeping over his boots, because a new question hit him in the face: Why did he keep using *they* in reference to Royce? She wasn't a class of people; she was one woman. Why was he thinking of her in the plural?

The answer came when he attempted to picture her, and what he saw in his mind's eye was Royce with blonde hair. Immediately he realized that he hadn't been thinking of—or living with, or arguing with—Royce herself, but this fictional amalgamation of Royce and Kris, who was blonde. Heck, there was probably thrown into the mix a little bit of every girl who had ever snubbed him.

So it became a self-fulfilling prophecy for Royce to leave him. Because Kris had left him, he started off his new marriage as if Royce was going to leave him, too. When he had alienated her to the point that she couldn't take it anymore, she left, thereby justifying not only his prescience but his status as stomped-on innocent male victim.

Paul folded his arms across his chest to prevent himself from violently puking. Then he saw something else: Streiker saw this.

By forcing Paul into the active role of searcher, he was simultaneously forcing him out of the passive role of victim. Whatever happened now would happen because Paul made it happen, not because he sat back and let things happen around him, or to him. If he found Royce and she rejected him, it would at least effect a resolution that he had sought. And from now on, whatever happened would be between him and Royce and no one else.

After reaching this noble conclusion, he suddenly wondered if he could get hold of Streiker and maybe convince him that he was ready for a shortcut in finding Royce. Paul pulled out his phone, toying with the keypad. Shouldn't a company as big as The Streiker Corporation have somebody answering the phone over the weekend?

He returned to the truck to pull out the crinkled interview sheet (and left both doors open to let the seat air out a bit). Noting the corporate number, he dialed it. When the recording came on, he almost terminated the call without hearing the whole thing. But for no other reason than to kill time, he listened, and at the end of the message, the recorded voice said, "If your call is urgent, please dial our after-hours number"—which was then given.

Paul memorized the number and quickly redialed, putting the phone to his ear. When a live voice came on the line—on a Sunday!—Paul was so astonished that he didn't say anything right away. "Hello?" the woman repeated.

He cleared his throat. "I'm sorry. My name is Paul Arrendondo. I'm trying to reach Mr. Streiker."

"Where are you calling from?" she asked.

"Fort Worth. Texas," he said.

"Ah. I'm sorry; Mr. Streiker is no longer stateside. He flew into Fort Worth yesterday for one appointment. Once he was through with that, he got back on a plane for Hawaii, where his wife and son live. About the most I can do for you now is forward a message," she said.

"Yeah, okay," he said, rubbing his eyes. "Please just —ask him to call." The request was so preposterous that the only way he could get it out was to say it without thinking about it. But what flashed across his mind was the feed store in San Angelo.

"Sure," she said.

He gave her his cell phone number, thanked her, and hung up. He replaced his phone in his pocket with a disappointed sigh. At least this lady was—actually, she was really nice about taking a message from him on a Sunday. Her job description probably didn't entail forwarding weekend messages from nobodies to the head of the corporation.

Dismally, Paul leaned against the truck beside the open door. Also, now that he thought about it, he was fortunate that Streiker somehow made time to catch him when he was in town for just one appointment—

Another one of those brick-wall insights hit him. Could it be—? Nah, that was impossible. It was absurd for Paul to think that Streiker would have flown in from Hawaii just to catch him at the mall and kick him in the seat several times. Surely Streiker was too busy to bother with one dimwit's personal problems. But . . . suppose he did? Crazy as it sounds, suppose Streiker flew in just to talk to him? Why on earth would he do that? How could he know—?

Paul looked out over the hot, faded greenness while repressing the sudden thumping of his heart. Streiker would know a lot if he had talked to Royce.

A whole bag of loose pieces suddenly fell into place. Even busy executives might take the time to get to know new hires. If the boss wanted to know why she was alone and friendless in a strange city, and she told him about her jackass husband whom she still loved, Streiker was the kind of man to see if said ass couldn't be led to a reconciliation by a bit between his teeth. But, if that was the case, it meant that Royce did want him back.

"Why wouldn't she just *call me*, then?" he muttered, exasperated. But even as he said it, he could see why she might not. After a month's absence, she wouldn't know how he felt—whether he'd be angry over her leaving; whether he was happy that she was gone; whether (as ludicrous as it sounded) he had found someone to take her place. So if she confessed these doubts to Streiker, it is entirely possible he would say something like, *"Well, let's see how badly he wants you back. Leave it to me."*

With new motivation, Paul closed the passenger door and hopped up into his truck. Leaving the park, he got a burger from a fast-food drive-through. After gulping it down, he drove around in mounting impatience. Did he have to wait till tomorrow to resume his search? Was there *anything* he could today?

Unexpectedly heavy traffic brought him to an idling standstill on an eight-lane thoroughfare. After ten minutes of creeping along, he saw the reason: he had driven unwittingly close to a mall entrance. Its shops and restaurants were open for business on Sunday just like any other day.

Paul looked out the side window at the stream of traffic flowing into the vast parking lots. Royce wasn't necessarily home watching baseball today. She could have a job that required some Sunday hours.

He then looked across the street at a branch of the Fort Worth Public Library system, also open for a few hours this afternoon. Glancing over his shoulder, he turned the wheel away from the mall parking into the left-hand lane of the thoroughfare, and from there U-turned. He hadn't gotten a master's degree without learning something about library research. But the branch wouldn't have what he needed; he would have to go downtown.

Twenty minutes later he was pulling up to the classical façade of the central library—a place he knew well from his college days. He parked and trotted up the steps to the front entrance, whipping off his sunglasses. Okay, not too crowded today. And a librarian sat at the information desk just waiting for him to walk up and ask her a question.

He did not disappoint her: "Hello. I need to do some research on The Streiker Corporation. I'd like to find out what businesses they have in Fort Worth."

"Certainly. I believe you'll find what you need back in Business and Periodicals." She pointed over her shoulder. "The librarian on duty will assist you."

"Ah. Thank you." He walked back to the section she indicated, and repeated his request to the assistant librarian. And over the next several hours, she walked him through the Dun & Bradstreet reports, *Hoover's Handbook of Private Companies*, Infotrac, Nexis, and a smattering of business journals.

By the time they were done, he walked out of the library with a list in hand of twelve Streiker subsidiaries that operated in the Fort Worth area—not a com-prehensive list, as probably nobody but the federal government knew the extent of Streiker's holdings. But it was enough to get started on, and Paul had by now worked himself up to the conviction that he was going to find her.

As he stepped into the hot glare of the parking lot, reaching for his sunglasses, his phone warbled so suddenly that it almost gave him heart failure. He whipped it out, looked at the display, and answered. "Hi, Buddy."

"Hi, Paul. Hey, uh, Ren and I were just wondering how it's going," Buddy said.

"Well, I—" Paul paused beside his truck, moving out of the way for another car to pull out. "I talked to Fletcher Streiker yesterday, and he told me that Royce is in Fort Worth. I think she's working for one of his companies."

"She is? That's great! Didn't he tell you which one?" Buddy asked.

"No, he didn't. I'm . . . not sure why. I tried to call him, but he flew back to Hawaii. Anyhow, I've got a list that I'm going to start hitting tomorrow. Listen—how are things at the ranch? How's Mama?"

"She's doing fine, Paul. Don't worry about her. Last I saw, my mom had sat her down with a list of chores yea long, and Juanita seemed glad to do them."

"Good. Ah, Joe get the cattle shipped out okay?" Paul asked.

"Yeah, they're all trucked out. I guess that was the right thing to do, even if Mom lost a little in the deal. I think it was a relief to her to get rid of them. Listen, we —Ren and I—left this afternoon. We're on our way to the airport now."

"You left already?" Paul asked in brotherly disapproval.

"Yeah." Buddy lowered his voice. "Ren and Mom got into a little discussion about how much we've been traveling since I decided not to go back to school. Mom seems to think we're blowing through my trust a little too—efficiently."

"Aren't you?" Paul snorted.

"Maybe," Buddy admitted.

Paul heard a rustling, as if Buddy was settling into a car seat. "Was it so bad that you had to leave right then?" Paul asked. "I mean . . . I thought your mom was kind of counting on you to help her sort through everything—"

"What was I supposed to do?" Buddy said defensively. "Ren said there was no way she was going let Mom run our lives like she did yours and Royce's."

Paul's latent resentment against Renetta reared up. "Oh, come on, it wasn't quite like that. Besides, I mean —how would Ren know? You weren't even there."

"Royce called her a couple times," Buddy said.

"Called her? When?" Paul demanded.

"Ah, I'm not sure. Seems like I remember her mentioning it a few weeks before she left."

Paul was stunned. "Royce called Renetta and you never thought of saying anything about it to me?"

"Look, I didn't want to—"

"Is Renetta there with you?" Paul asked.

"Yes. You want to talk to her?"

"If you don't mind," Paul said, stinging. Since this conversation seemed to be drawing itself out, he moved to the shade of a maple tree presiding over the patch of grass next to the parking lot.

He heard Renetta's voice: "Hello?"

"Ren, when—when did you talk to Royce?" Paul sputtered.

"Well—" Renetta cleared her throat. "I don't remember, exactly, Paul. I think it was in June."

"What did she say?"

"She complained a lot about Jeannine, and not being able to go anywhere or do anything. I assumed it was something you'd already heard, because when I told her she needed to tell you about it, she said she did. So I thought she just needed to vent," Renetta said.

Paul exhaled, hanging his head. "Yes, she told me, and I wasn't listening."

"Well, there's something else you should know," Renetta began.

He heard Buddy's voice objecting in the background. Paul asked, "What? What's he saying?"

Muffled sounds followed, and snatches of a muted argument. Paul wiped sweat from the side of his face and folded his free arm across his chest. "Renetta? Buddy?"

She came back on the line. "Here's one reason we left the ranch: I talked to Shana, and she said Royce called for you, and Jeannine told her not to tell you."

7

"What?" Paul gasped. "Royce called?"

Buddy came back on the line. "Okay, Paul—we don't know that. After Ren told me this, I talked to Shana, and, she's—not real bright, you know, and sometimes she just makes stuff up. Somebody did call for you a couple of weeks ago, and I think what happened was that you were out in the pasture with Dad, and Shana just forgot to go back to the phone and take a message. I asked Mom about it, and she had no idea what I was talking about. She would never do something like that—you know that, Paul. It tore her up almost as much as you when Royce left."

Paul wiped his watering eyes. "Could it have been Royce, Buddy? Assuming that it happened like you say?"

"Yeah, I suppose it could've been," Buddy admitted. "But Mom would never lie about it like that. Shana might."

"Okay," Paul exhaled. He steadied himself with a hand on the tree. "Okay. Where're you going now?"

"Back to New York City for a few weeks. Ren's got

some friends she wants to look up," Buddy said. "Look —keep us posted, okay?"

"Sure. I'll call." Paul closed his phone and climbed back in his truck to turn on the air conditioning. "Get a grip," he muttered, still reeling from the likely fact that she did call, and he never got the message. That, too, explained a lot: she would assume he didn't talk to her because he didn't want to talk to her, so she never called back.

This revelation galvanized his resolve to find her. And if he ran out of cash, he'd just find some drug dealers to rob.

But today was still Sunday, and he was restless to get started on the next phase of his search. So he decided to waste gas driving around to some of these places on his list. Pulling out the sheet, he asterisked those that were downtown (closest to where he was now)—four of the twelve.

Downtown employment made sense for a nondriver, as light rail and bus service ran all over Fort Worth from the downtown hub. It would be even more likely for her to rent a downtown apartment or loft close enough to walk to work. Once you got used to evading the panhandlers, it was a thrill not to have to commute any distance to your job.

As Paul started up the truck and headed toward his first destination, he thought back to his acceptance of a counselor position at Ville du Havre, a drug treatment hospital in downtown Dallas. This was after the DEA put an end to the robberies shortly before he and Royce were married.

She had been pleased with this prospect, even

though it didn't pay much. But the more he had thought about working in downtown Dallas, the less appeal the job held for him—which had not been much to begin with. So by the time Walt broached the possibility of Paul's staying on at the ranch, he jumped at the chance without considering any other options. The Ferrings made it as palatable as they could for Royce, too; it wasn't anyone's fault that Walt's heart gave out. Sure wasn't *Paul's* fault.

He turned the wheel, deliberately turning away from recriminations. It was a bad habit to blame himself for everything that went wrong. And assuming he *was* to blame for anything here, the only way to make it right was to do what he was doing now. Beating himself up at the same time didn't help at all.

Glancing down at his notes, he bypassed a one-way street to turn down the next. The first place on his list was an art gallery in the entertainment district. Here, Paul's intuitive knowledge of his hometown kicked in; he located the gallery quickly, even though he'd never been to it before.

When he pulled up, he was mildly surprised to see cars in the modest parking lot: The gallery was open. He parked and climbed out of his truck, deliberating what to say. Trying to formulate an opening speech paralyzed him, so he shook his head and walked on in. The only way to successfully improvise, he was discovering, was not to think too much, and just tell the truth—but as little of it as he could get by with.

The building was a rustic southwestern stucco design, bright in the hot sun; entering by the glass door, he found the silent air conditioning to be operating at peak efficiency, which made the inside of the building enormously more comfortable than it looked from the outside. Paul removed his sunglasses and glanced around the front showroom: mostly paintings, mostly of southwestern landscapes and architecture. There was a room on his left showcasing sculptures and a room on his right with textiles and jewelry.

Ten or twelve patrons browsed the displays while the solitary clerk (that he saw) discussed the merits of an early John Paul Strain with another potential customer. It was most certainly an upper-end gallery, not the kind of place a ranch hand would feel comfortable in, unless as a subject.

Paul stopped in front of a portrait of a grizzled rancher sitting on a split-rail fence. Yes, he could see Royce working here—she'd love the realism of the portrait without the subject's disagreeable body odor or tobacco spittle everywhere. Paul glanced at the price tag: $2500. Definitely, Royce would feel at home here.

Idly perusing the art, he wandered toward the back of the gallery, where he saw a door with the discreet sign: "Employees Only." His happy accident at Gold Cord colored his hopes here, although he did not really believe that he could waltz back into this office and burgle their employee files.

Another gallery employee, previously unseen, approached him. She was in her early thirties, tall and slender, with sleek, dark hair, meticulous makeup, and tasteful dress—the kind of woman who naturally intimidated Paul.

He turned to feign scrutiny of the painting closest to him. Standing in front of it as well, she said, "Isn't it lovely? That's an area artist, Pam Taylor. She's gained quite a following."

So he actually looked at the painting, and the label next to it that said, "Santa Elena Canyon." "I've been there," he murmured, studying the tawny cliffs littered with car-sized boulders at their base. The painting rendered the one side of the canyon in stark light, the other in deep shadow, the muddy river meandering between them, and the achingly blue sky behind. "It breaks your heart."

"Yes," she said quietly. "I think she captures that feeling well, don't you?"

Paul glanced at the price tag, which indicated $1200. "Better than I can afford," he remarked. "Anyway," he said, turning to her, "I'm not really here to look at the art —though it's a very nice gallery. I—want to leave a message for Royce Arrendondo. I'm her husband, Paul. We're separated. She called at the ranch where I was working a few weeks ago, but I never got the message till just now. I don't know her new phone number and she doesn't know that I didn't get her message."

The woman listened with red lips slightly parted. "Does . . . your ex-wife—what was her name?"

"Royce. We're still married," Paul said.

"Does Royce have some connection with this gallery?"

"I'm pretty sure she's working at one of Streiker's companies—I talked to him yesterday, and he told me she's in Fort Worth," Paul explained.

"He didn't tell you which company?" she asked dubiously.

"No," Paul said. "He encouraged me to look for her,

but he didn't tell me where." At her skeptical look, he said, "It didn't make any sense to me, either." While this was something of a misstatement, he felt it unwise to attempt further explanation. He kept reminding himself not to talk too much—she would have decided within the first five seconds whether to help him or not.

"Well," she said with delicately arched brow, "All I can tell you is that she doesn't work here. But this is what I'll do—is there a number where we can reach you in the next few days?"

"Yes," he said, whipping out his pen. "Do you have any paper?"

"Here." She went to a counter and pulled out a scratch pad.

He wrote his name and cell number, then added the note, "looking for Royce Arrendondo."

As he handed the pad back to her, she said, "I'll search the employee banks of The Streiker Corporation and see if I find her. If I do, I'll look her up and give her your message. All right?"

"Yes, that'd be great. Miss—?" he hinted, extending a hand.

"Miriam," she said (which was printed on her employee name tag. Either he didn't see it, or was fishing for a last name). She accepted his hand to lightly shake it.

"Miriam. Thank you. I really appreciate it," he said earnestly.

"You're welcome," she nodded. Retrieving his sunglasses from his pocket, he turned and walked outside.

Miriam watched through the window as he climbed

into his truck. He started the engine and sat there a minute, and she waited till he drove off.

Then she went back to the employee-only area. Standing over a desk, she picked up the phone and paused, her brow wrinkling in concentration. "Oh, I can't remember it," she muttered.

So she took a purse from the desk drawer. Digging through it, she finally extracted a card from which she dialed a number. She waited as if listening to a message, then said, "Royce, this is Miriam. Your husband just came by the gallery looking for you. I didn't tell him anything, but I took his number, if you want it."

Before leaving the parking lot of the art gallery, Paul brought out his battered sheet and checked off number one on his list, feeling faintly hopeful. This lady seemed sincere in her offer, so, if she was able to locate Royce, and actually gave her his message, he stood a chance of hearing from her.

Destination Number Two on his list of downtown Streiker-owned companies was a bookstore, prosaically named The Old Book Shoppe, only about four blocks away from the art gallery. Pulling into its crowded lot to park, Paul deduced that they did a robust Sunday-afternoon business. He surveyed the Tudor-style building before entering the wooden front door and removing his sunglasses.

While the air conditioning here was also efficient, the comfort of the interior seemed to derive mostly from its Old World ambience: wood, dark fabrics, soft lighting. From what he could ascertain in a three-minute survey, the large floor space was broken up by bookshelves into a maze of corridors and reading niches appointed with old-fashioned lamps, overstuffed chairs, whimsical footstools, and, in one corner, a play area for children. The windows were frosted diamond panes, and a few boasted stained-glass pictures of medieval scenes. Paul stopped, mildly startled, in front of a full suit of armor on display at the end of one row of shelves.

Turning to the rough-plastered wall on his left, he regarded a large painting of a caped, helmeted hero on horseback attacking a winged serpent with a toothpick-like sword. The body parts of previous victims lay scattered around the creature. Despite the deficiency of the weapon, the serpent was already vanquished, being trampled by the horse. In attendance, of course, was the crowned princess, hands clasped in gratitude to her brave rescuer. The brass label on the frame of the reproduction read, "Sodoma: St. George and the Dragon, ca. 1505-18."

Although Paul was not particularly sensitive to art, for the second time in one day he found himself responding on a visceral level to a painting. Great themes, like love and rescue, were eternal. This—this hero on horseback—is what he wanted to be for Royce. Was that possible, at this point?

He turned away, troubled, to make his way down an aisle. Given the number of people here (as indicated by the cars in the parking lot) it was interesting that nobody seemed to be getting in anyone else's way. That must be due partly to the strange layout: There were a lot of books, for sure, but they were arranged more like a graduate library than a store. The number of small reading areas contributed to the feeling of being in a private club—one to which you belonged.

Also, there were a lot of idiosyncratic knickknacks that seemed to dangerously invite handling. Everywhere he looked, there was something unusual to stare at: a branch with a lifelike replica of a tree frog. A model of the Ptolemaic universe as used in Dante's *Divine Comedy*. A display of medieval wax document seals, open to touching.

The seals caught his attention for some reason. He bent to study reproductions of the seal of Matilda, queen of Henry I, 1100-18 . . . Idonea de Hurst, late twelfth century . . . Joan de Stuteville, 1265-75: "An unusual seal in many respects. Unlike the normal seal of a lady— a standing figure in a pointed oval—it is round and shows her on horseback, riding sidesaddle. Instead of a hawk she carries a shield, and though Joan had two husbands the arms on the shield are her father's, probably to emphasise her position as his sole heiress." *So*, Paul mused in faint humor, *wimmin have been high-minded and independent for a lot longer that I thought.*

He straightened in mild wonder. This bookstore was more like a hands-on museum, a visual, tactile prod to the imagination. And everything looked old: no computers, cash registers, advertising, or sale tables. The only sign he saw—and he saw it everywhere—said, "If you don't find what you're looking for, ASK."

He wandered up one aisle and down another, ostensibly looking for an employee, but he kept getting sidetracked by the store's merchandise. In one niche, he came upon an empty reading chair which he narrowly avoided sitting in. On the side table were three or four books left carelessly out; the topmost was Virgil's *Aeneid*.

Without conscious thought, Paul picked it up. He had begun reading this book—devouring it—the summer before he started seminary. But he had stopped without finishing it, because something about it rattled him, creating all kinds of doubts about what he was doing. He had to go to seminary; his father was dead set on it, but fifteen years later Paul knew it had been a colossal mistake. Something in this book had been whispering that to him, so he had put it down, unable to face the truth at the time.

Standing beside the chair now, he flipped it open at random and read:

Whoever you are, I doubt Heaven is unfriendly
To you, as you still breathe life-giving air
On your approach to the Tyrian town. Go on:
Betake yourself this way to the queen's gate.

"Find what you're looking for?" a friendly voice asked.

Paul quickly looked up, replacing the book on the side table. A twenty-something guy in glasses and checkered shirt regarded him attentively. Paul spilled out, "Actually—I was looking for Royce Arrendondo."

"Oh, she's off today," the guy nodded.

Paul lowered his head, swallowing to dislodge his heart from his throat. Straining to keep his voice light, he said, "Ah. Do you know if she works tomorrow?"

"She'd better, 'cause I'm off," he replied with a snort.

"Okay, well, I'll drop back by then. Thanks," Paul said, and casually sauntered back to the front door. On the way out, he glanced up—hanging over the doorway was a large framed reproduction of Botticelli's "Primavera." The three Graces, dressed in rippling, translucent gauze, danced directly over his head. That the girl on the left resembled Royce both disturbed and excited him.

He left the parking lot immediately so he would not seem to be loitering, but he was so distracted that he almost ran right up over a curb. So he found another parking lot to stop and just breathe for a minute.

He turned off the engine, cranked down the window, and sat. Wiping his mouth, he looked over his wrinkled page of notes that represented Lord knows how many hours of research. The original list of treatment centers that Mitch had given him lay discarded on the floorboard. He could hardly believe that in just 24 hours, he had found her.

Wait a minute. As usual, he was leaping ahead of himself. He had not yet found her; he had found where she worked. If she figured out that he was looking for her and didn't want to be found, she could make herself inaccessible without leaving town. All she had to do was file for a restraining order.

Paul looked out the window over the concrete, shimmering in the afternoon heat. Now that he had unearthed an actual point of contact, he was afraid. What if she didn't want to see him? What if she told him to get lost? The possibility caused all connective tissues in his body to snap, leaving his limbs lying uselessly around his trunk.

But Streiker told me to look for her, he argued, struggling to pull himself together. *He talked to her. He knows how she feels. So he wouldn't goad me on a wild goose chase.* Would he?

The buttinski, Paul suddenly thought, growing angry. What business was it of Streiker's? Who asked him to—

Another thought derailed that one: What if Royce had gone to *him*? What if *she* had asked for his help?

Paul tried to sort through the repercussions of this thought, but it was like trying to corral a flood of ping-pong balls. *Okay, I'm almost certain she talked to him. So if she went to him for help, then it means she wants to see me.*

Maybe, his cynical side replied. What if she went to Streiker and said, *"I left the Ferrings' ranch without saying goodbye, and last time I called, my husband wouldn't talk to me. How do I make a clean break with him so I can start my life over?"*

So Streiker talks to Paul and tells him to go look for her, giving him just enough information to find her. With just enough difficulty inherent in the quest to keep him interested, he succeeds. Thus primed to listen, he hears her grievances, agrees he is a jackass, and they part amicably. What if the whole point of this exercise is to free her? What if he's not the knight, but the dragon in the picture?

Almost nauseous, Paul laid his head on the steering wheel. Then he suddenly sat up. "All right, I'm not going to do this to myself. If Royce doesn't want to see me, she can tell me so, but I'm not gonna defeat myself before I even get started."

With that issue resolved, he realized that he was tired and hungry. So, starting up the truck, he began casting around for someplace to eat and someplace to sleep. There were a lot of hotels downtown, but most of them were beyond his straitened means, so these he passed by.

As he drove around, he became uneasily aware of the number of vehicles clogging the streets—highly unusual for late Sunday afternoon. The preponderance of out-of-state license plates and erratic driving alerted him to the fact that something was going on downtown that might monopolize other facilities besides the streets. Therefore, he'd better secure lodging for the night before he had dinner.

So he pulled up to a mid-range hotel and entered the lobby, carrying his suitcases. Finding himself at the end of a long line to the check-in counter, he dropped his bags with a sigh, kicking them along as he slowly advanced. (An infrequent flier, he did not have luggage with wheels. He doubted that he would ever, at any point in his life, purchase luggage with wheels.) After fifteen minutes, he attained the front spot, and a harried desk clerk barked, "Reservation number?"

"I don't have a reservation," Paul began, pulling out his wallet.

"Then we can't help you," she returned. "Next!"

"But—wait a minute, can't you find—"

"Sir, we're booked solid, and overbooked. I'm sorry. Next!" She leaned around him and the next patron laid his credit card on the counter.

Thus booted, Paul retreated with his bags out to his truck. He drove south out of downtown, searching for likely vacancies, then stopped at a lower-end motel. Before hauling out his bags, he went inside unencumbered to make sure he could get a room.

That the small, dreary lobby was crowded was not a good sign. After waiting in line again, Paul got up to the desk to say, "I need a room for the night, but I don't have a reservation."

The lone clerk glanced at him while filling out another customer's credit slip. "Sorry. We're all booked."

"What is going on?" Paul asked in frustration.

"Friend, you need to get happy!" the visitor beside him said, pocketing his charge slip.

Paul eyed him. "I would be happy if I could get a room for the night."

"No, that's what's going on," the fellow said, grinning. "It's the Get Happy Conference—ten thousand people all in one place singing and shouting and praising the Lord!"

Paul turned to him. "I'll praise the Lord if you let me sleep in your room on a cot tonight."

"Fat chance," the fellow said, still smiling, and bent for his suitcase.

The next customer elbowed past Paul to present his reservation number at the counter, so Paul returned to his truck. While evening descended, he considered his options. He could drive around all night looking for a room in the Fort Worth area, or he could just stop at every motel between here and Dallas till he found one, but after getting so close to locating Royce, he couldn't abide the thought of retreating for lack of lodging. It was possible—not wise, but possible—to pull over somewhere and just sleep in his truck. He seriously considered this before visualizing himself meeting her tomorrow reeking of yesterday's sweat. He needed a shower even more than a bed.

Resting his head in his hand, Paul exhaled wearily. What was he supposed to do now? How could he . . . ? The complaint faded as he remembered something. In sudden concentration, he retrieved from the floorboard his list of Streiker-owned companies in Fort Worth. And he saw that number eight on that list was a bed and breakfast in south Fort Worth—not far from where he sat now. He mulled over this a minute, then decided nothing ventured, nothing gained. So he cranked up the truck to drive on over to the bed and breakfast.

It was a large old mansion in an historic area of the city. As Paul expected, its asphalt parking lot was crammed with vehicles, so he had to park down the street a ways. He emerged from his truck in slight despair, then, in a show of faith, hauled out both suitcases to carry with him.

There was—surprise, surprise—a line in the front parlor, which he took to be the check-in area. So, with his bags, Paul waited patiently until his turn came at the desk, behind which sat a young woman with an old-fashioned ledger. He quietly asked, "May I see the manager, please?"

She looked mildly startled, then picked up her phone and murmured into it. Paul considerately stepped out of the way so that she could attend the next person in line while he waited.

A moment later the door of a room behind the desk opened, and a large, graying woman exited to approach the desk. "Mrs. Nicholas, this gentleman asked to see you," the girl gestured with her pen.

Paul extended his hand. "Paul Arrendondo."

"Mr. Arrendondo." She shook his hand and paused.

"May we talk in private?" he asked.

She appraised him at a glance. "Come back to the office," she said, indicating the room she had come from. He picked up his bags and followed her. "Please have a seat." She nodded to a chair across from a cluttered desk as she sat herself, having left the door open.

"Thank you." Paul set his bags down beside the chair and sat. "Mrs. Nicholas"—he swallowed—"I'm in town on an . . . errand that Fletcher Streiker encouraged me to—undertake. I need a room for the night, but, obviously, every place in the area is full up. I'm sure you are, too. I am asking if—you can find a corner for me anywhere. All I need is a place to sleep and a place to shower. I wouldn't be so presumptuous to come ask you this except for the fact that Mr. Streiker is—somewhat—responsible for my being here at all, so . . . can you help me?"

She shifted. "I'm not sure. The first question that comes to mind, Mr. Arrendondo, is, how do I know that you have anything to do with Mr. Streiker?"

Paul sagged slightly. "That's a reasonable question, Mrs. Nicholas. He's—not even in town; he flew back to Hawaii. But—maybe I can get him to verify that for you."

He pulled out his phone to display his recent calls, the last of which was the Streiker Corporation night number. "Excuse me for a moment," he said, dialing, and she nodded, returning to the paperwork on her desk.

Tense, he listened to the phone ring on the other end. Then, to his immense relief, the same woman answered that he had talked to before: "Hello?"

8

*P*aul quickly cleared his throat. "Um, hello, this is Paul Arrendondo again. I was sure hoping to hear from Mr. Streiker."

"I'm sorry; he's still out of pocket," the woman on the other end replied.

"Hmm. Well, I'm in a bit of a bind. I'm—trying to do what he suggested, but I'm stuck in Fort Worth without a room for the night. Right now I'm at the York Bed and Breakfast, trying to convince Mrs. Nicholas to give me a couch to sleep on," Paul rambled.

"I see. Why don't you put her on?" the woman suggested.

"Sure," Paul said, and blankly held out his phone. "She wants to talk to you."

The woman glanced up and took his cell phone. "This is Mrs. Nicholas. . . . Oh, hello, Yvonne; how are you? How's that boy? No, really? What is he doing now?"

Dazed, Paul listened to five minutes of one-sided feminine chit-chat before she said, "Now, what I am supposed to do with Mr. Arrendondo? . . . Um hmm.

Um hmm. I see. Well, it's good to talk to you. When are you going to be in town? Oh, then, do stop by. All right, then. Bye."

She handed him back his phone, which he closed and replaced in his pocket. With a faint grunt, she stood from behind the desk; he watched her like a dog waiting to be walked. "Excuse me for just a moment," she said, and left the office. He twisted in the chair to see her stand at the outer desk for a minute, then leave the parlor altogether. Paul turned back to sit in the chair, sweating, half wondering if the cops would show up next.

Some minutes later she returned, and he bolted up. She held out an old-fashioned key to him. "All right, Mr. Arrendondo, you're in the Baron's Closet on the third floor—up the stairs to your right, next-to-last room at the end of the hall. It's a small room, I'm afraid, and it shares a bath with the south third-floor wing, but that's the best I can do for you on such short notice."

"Thank you," he said, taking the key. "I—really, thank you so much. I've got—" he started digging in his back pocket for his wallet—"I'm not sure if I've hit the limit on this card, but I should have enough cash—"

She was reseating herself behind the desk. "Your room bill has been provided for, Mr. Arrendondo, as are your meals. I believe the buffet is still open in the dining room." She pointed over her shoulder with her pen.

He stuttered, "Why—thank you. I'm just a little—who was that on the phone?"

She eyed him in mild amusement. "That was Yvonne Fay."

"Well—that was really nice of her. I don't know her, or why she would bother about me," he said, distracted.

"She is Mr. Streiker's personal assistant. He must have talked to her about you, since she was able to basically verify what you told me," she said, returning to the work on her desk.

Streiker's personal assistant? Paul had gotten hold of Streiker's personal assistant by calling the night number? He steadied himself on the chair, then leaned forward with outstretched hand over her desk. "Thank you again, Mrs. Nicholas. You are a jewel."

"Certainly," she smiled, laying aside the pen to shake his hand. He bent for his bags, but she gestured, "Those will be taken up to your room. I'd head for the buffet now, if I were you."

He paused in the doorway. "I know I'm repeating myself, but . . . thank you." She eyed him, still smiling.

Shortly, Paul found his way to the door of a cozy, sumptuous dining room, with a total of eight tables scattered lovingly in the space. On the far end of the room, the caterer was indeed clearing away the buffet dishes, so Paul hurried over to grab a plate and beg spoonfuls of whatever was left. Within sixty seconds, he was sitting at a table with a smorgasbord of roast beef, mashed potatoes and gravy, cranberries, broccoli, bread, and peach cobbler.

A waitress brought her last customer of the evening iced tea. Apologetically, she also laid the check beside his plate. "Um, I really need to take off. You can just sign your name and room. Do you need anything else?"

"No, thanks," he said. Taking her pen, he wrote his name and, absently, "Broom Closet" on the check. She took it and turned away while he picked up his fork. Then he jumped up. "Wait!"

She looked back curiously; he pulled out his wallet and handed her a ten. Her eyes widened. "Gosh. Thanks."

He sat again, grunting, "Just wanted to hear somebody else besides me say it." She smiled at him over her shoulder and he industriously set to demolishing the roast beef.

When he had cleared half the plate and began to slow down, he reached into his shirt pocket for his phone. Scrolling through the recently called numbers, he paused, a shadow of curiosity crossing his face. He found The Streiker Corporation's main number and dialed it. He listened to the message again, through to the very end. Then he studied the phone as if it had changed colors on him.

Mystified, he dialed again, reaching the same recording. He listened very hard, until the message played out and the line went dead. But, as before, no night number was given. That part of the message had been deleted.

Slowly, Paul replaced the phone in his pocket and stared at empty space. He hadn't dreamed up the after-hours number—he had been able to reach Streiker's personal assistant at that number both times he called. But now that he had it, the number was no longer available to the public. . . . Paul finished his dinner in the dim, quiet room with his head down, deep in thought.

After a very satisfying meal, he emerged back into the softly lit parlor, now cleared of visitors. The front doors were locked for the night; everyone had either been given a room or turned away.

Touching the key in his pocket for reassurance, Paul

found the graceful, curving stairway and trotted all the way up to the third floor. From this landing, he turned right, as instructed. Globed yellow lights in the corridor enabled him to read the brass plates on the doors that he passed: "Bishop's Room," "Duke's Room," "Knight's Room," and so on, till he came to "Baron's Closet."

Inserting the key in the lock, Paul opened the door into a room that was indeed small—perhaps ten by twelve feet. There was a single bed with a side table, a dresser, a wash stand, and his two suitcases on the floor next to a wardrobe against the wall. First thing, Paul opened the wardrobe, fully expecting to see a snowy forest and a street lamp. But it was empty, except for a laundry bag (with instructions) hanging on the back of the door. "Wow. Laundry service. That's nice," he murmured.

He closed the wardrobe and glanced around again. Obviously, the room was dubbed a "closet" because there was no window, but that bothered him not at all. It looked so cozy that Paul almost dropped right onto the bed.

But first, he backed out into the hall to further explore until he had located the bathroom. It was very nice: tiled, with a claw-footed tub and hand-shower, fluffy beige towels and scented soap. Since no one was using these facilities at the moment, Paul returned to his room to hastily rummage through one suitcase for clean clothes. These he brought back to the bathroom to take a quick shower. He cleaned up after himself, then let himself back into the Baron's Closet and stretched out on the bed with a grateful sigh.

He awoke at 5:30 the following morning. When he

was able to focus on the lighted dial of his watch to see what time it was, he groaned and rolled over, trying to go back to sleep. But he couldn't; he was wired. Royce should be coming in to work today.

He lay on his back, hand on his forehead, staring into the darkness. The only light in the room was the dim strip that showed under the door from the hallway. What time would she be coming in? What time did the bookstore open? He had forgotten to check before leaving yesterday—probably not before ten. So he had four and a half hours to kill before he could even walk in the door.

Paul bunched the pillow under his head and determinedly closed his eyes, but it was futile. He was awake. Exhaling, he sat up, clicking on the bedside light. The brochure on the same little table promised a breakfast buffet beginning at 6:30, which was nice. Eating was a good way to pass the time. So, given ten minutes to shave and dress, he only had to while away 50 minutes till then. With nothing to look at, he turned the light off again. Maybe he could fool himself into falling back asleep if he pretended he was going to stay awake until breakfast.

He leaned back against the headboard, wishing he had bought that copy of *The Aeneid* yesterday. He would like to start reading it again. As a matter of fact, he'd probably get it today, since Streiker was covering his lodging—

For how long? he suddenly wondered. He'd better clarify with Mrs. Nicholas how long his stay was covered. Would Royce come back here with him, just for a night? Smiling, he ran a hand over six inches of mattress. They'd need a bigger room, with a bigger bed. He closed his eyes, leaning his head back again. Now he missed her. He sure took for granted that slender body tucked up next to his at night. He wished . . . he hadn't been so tired all the time.

Would she believe him that Walt's death changed everything? He opened his eyes again. Did Walt's death change everything? Could he assure her that he wouldn't repeat the pattern of their life at the ranch elsewhere?— that he wouldn't find another vocation that absorbed him to the point of excluding her?

That's a big reason he got burned out at the center. After being fired from the church, that was the only meaningful job he could find, so he was determined to make it count. (Until Walt hired him full-time last year, working at the ranch had been a part-time, weekend release.) The drug treatment center became his new vocation, his new ministry. And he so completely poured himself into the black hole of the addicts' self-destruction that there was nothing left of him.

Thinking back further, he realized that this was also partly to blame for his failure in the ministry—yes, his wife had left him, but mostly because she just couldn't accept the self-annihilation that went along with his pastoral work. Living in a fishbowl, the target of every church member's scrutiny, criticism, and demands, she finally rebelled—in a hurtful, unprofitable way, true, but . . . what options had he left open to her?

Paul looked through the darkness, seeing back to the past with a clarity he had not experienced before. He saw how even the counseling he had offered Kris had been stacked against her, being with a fellow pastor who had already told her that her station in life was basically fixed. Years later Paul heard that he, too, had divorced after his numerous affairs came to light. So it really should not have been such a surprise when Kris arranged for Paul to find her in bed with another man. It was her escape hatch from a one-sided marriage.

He looked to the side, in another direction, toward the future. Now that he had left the ranch, was what he going to do for a paycheck? He had just kind of assumed that he would tell Royce he would go wherever she wanted, take any job that would suit her needs—in other words, switch places to that of the inconsequential partner. Would she want that in a husband? Was there no middle ground between tyrant and doormat?

Paul sat up, leaning over to switch the light on again. He needed to approach her with a plan, at least—offer her some valid options to accept, reject, or modify. He needed a job. Scrambling out of bed, he flipped open a suitcase. He had one suit in here, but it was badly wrinkled by now, as were his dress shirts. He had accumulated some dirty clothes, as well. . . .

All these he gathered up, then opened the wardrobe door to retrieve the laundry bag. Paul wrote his name and room name on it (as per instructions), stuffed it with the clothes that needed attention, and hung it on the inside of his room door. Then he shaved in his room, using the old-fashioned wash stand and mirror. When he was all dressed, he went on downstairs.

The breakfast buffet was still twenty minutes away, but Paul turned to the front parlor, where a row of newspapers sat waiting for the guests' attention. The papers—some Sunday editions, some Monday—were from cities across the United States. Paul picked up the Fort Worth paper, dislodging the classifieds section. Still standing, he leafed through it to the employment ads. These he perused until the dining room doors opened; he wrote down a couple of addresses on some scrap paper he retrieved from the trash, then he folded the newspaper and replaced it as it had been.

He enjoyed a superior breakfast of ham and eggs, coffee and strawberries, then returned to the front parlor to sit down with the employment classifieds again. He studied the job openings thoroughly, taking notes on his scrap paper. Then, a few minutes before eight o'clock, he folded the paper back on the table and headed for the door.

Seeing the desk clerk take her place, Paul detoured toward her. When she looked up, he said, "I'm—Paul Arrendondo, in the Baron's Closet. Please tell Mrs. Nicholas that I really appreciate the room on such short notice, and I was wondering how long I would have use of it."

She knitted her brows in thought. "As long as you need it, as far as I know, though we'd like to have notice when you're checking out."

"Right. As soon as I know, I'll tell you," he said, then resumed his exit. He walked to his truck under a heavy weight of humility for Streiker's graciousness.

But right now Paul had work to do. Putting on his sunglasses (for the morning was already very bright), he checked his scrap paper with addresses, then started up the engine and the air conditioner and turned the wheel toward the first address on the list.

Thirty minutes later (given rush-hour traffic) he

pulled up to a branch office of Worldwide Delivery Services in a strip shopping center. He parked and entered, removing his sunglasses to glance around the clean, cool mailing facility.

As he made his way to the counter in the back, an attendant in shirt sleeves glanced up. "What can I do for you?"

"I'd like to apply for a position as a driver," Paul said, reaching into his back pocket for his wallet with his driver's license.

"Sure. Can you fill out an application on computer?" the guy asked.

"Yes," Paul said.

"Great. Have a seat there." The clerk pointed to a desk against the wall with a keyboard and monitor. "Hit any key, and the application will come up."

"Right." Paul sat before the monitor, brought up the application, and began filling in blanks on screen.

He gave all information possible, given his uncertain living situation, then saved it as instructed and returned to the back counter. The clerk then called up his application on the monitor there to glance through it.

Paul, feeling the need to head off the disqualification of being overqualified, began, "I do have a master's degree, but, I don't want to leave the impression—"

"Oh, no problem. We get seminary students all the time," the clerk said, glancing up from an emerging printout. "We're thinking of changing our company name to Heaven and Earth Delivery Services."

Paul laughed, and the guy handed him the printout. "Okay. We have to do the standard background check. You take that to the lab on McCart—address is there at the top—and pee in a cup, and then come back in—can you start on Wednesday?"

"Wednesday." In two days. "Yeah, sure."

"Okay, see you then. We got your phone number?" the clerk asked, glancing back to the monitor.

"My cell, yeah. I'm married to it," Paul replied.

The clerk laughed, and Paul turned out with a little heartache.

McCart was a long, winding street, so Paul had to drive quite a ways to locate the lab. Once there, he presented Worldwide Delivery Services' request for a drug test on himself. He was handed a plastic cup and shown to a restroom, where he produced the required sample.

Following the labeling of his sample, the lab technician asked him the standard questions about what medications he was taking (none), whether he smoked (no), and what he'd had to eat or drink in the last 24 hours (nothing stronger than beer. "Any poppy seed cake?" "Poppy seed? No.").

By the time he left the lab, it was ten minutes after ten o'clock. So Paul turned the wheel with clammy hands back toward The Old Book Shoppe downtown. He drove with all due care in the heavy traffic, but other drivers, unaware of the preoccupation weighing on him, kept irrationally honking their horns at him or extending a certain finger to his view.

Finally, he pulled up to The Old Book Shoppe without serious incident, and cut the engine. He sat there for a moment, looking over the other cars in the parking lot. Was one of these hers? There were only three. Somewhat deviously, Paul flipped over his scrap and wrote down the make, model and license-plate number of all three cars. Then he climbed out of his truck and shakily entered the cool interior of the bookstore, removing his sunglasses.

He stood at the front of the store, just breathing a minute, but it was very quiet—certainly much less crowded than it had been yesterday afternoon. Thus stabilized, he was looking around for the checkout counter when a thought occurred to him.

He wandered up and down the aisles until he found the niche where he had left *The Aeneid* sitting on the table—there it was. Taking possession of the book, he carried it back to the front of the store, looking around all the while for an employee to assist him. Tucked in the front right corner, almost obscured by the surrounding architecture, was a counter at which a lone employee sat. Swallowing, Paul laid the book on the counter.

Without looking up, she glanced at the cover and rang up the sale on an antique cash register. "That's ten ninety-five," she said, and Paul handed her cash. While she made change, he eyed the entrance to the employees-only room behind her.

As she dropped the change in his hand, he cleared his throat and said, "Is Royce in today?"

"No, she called in sick, and left me here by myself," the girl said angrily.

Paul looked at her. "May I leave a message for her?"

"Sure," she shrugged.

He paused. "May I have something to write it down?"

Sighing, she rummaged on the counter for blank

paper, which she shoved toward him. Paul took out his pen and hesitantly wrote, "Royce. Walt died and I left the ranch. I'm getting a job ~~here~~ in FtW. Please call. Paul." He added his phone number, although she should have it, and handed the note to the cashier. Then he turned and walked out.

She watched him go in mild surprise, then noticed the book still on the counter. "Wait! You forgot—" But he was out the door.

He went directly to his truck and pulled out of the lot, then drove aimlessly until he came to himself to see that he was in his old neighborhood, at the head of the street where his parents' condemned house sat. This being the last place on earth Paul wanted to be right now, it seemed inevitable for him to be here. He turned the corner and pulled up to the ramshackle structure.

Slowly climbing out of the truck to mount the front steps, he saw a new demolition notice on the door which insisted that tomorrow was the day this pile of rotting, termite-infested timber was coming down. Paul pocketed his sunglasses and opened the door to go in.

He passed through the front room with the sagging sofa and the moth-eaten Last Supper wall hanging; the dust and dimness followed him into the kitchen, where the old white appliances sat as if embalmed, awaiting burial. The floor creaked under his step; the asbestos-laden linoleum puckered upon his passing through his parents' tiny bedroom to the children's bedroom at the back. One metal-framed bed with a stinking, discolored mattress remained. There was no bath.

Paul sat on the edge of the mattress, remembering unhappy years of wrestling with siblings over space.

Growing up, he soon discovered as sisters multiplied and new babies kept intruding, that the only way to find any peace was to escape to the tiny, weedy backyard. Most nights he slept out there, looking up at the stars; when it was cold and rainy, he slept in a torn tent he had found in the trash. He would rather be cold than crowded. He'd rather be alone.

So that was it. She knew he was looking for her, so she called in sick to avoid him. But Royce was smart; she knew that it was a temporary escape. Right now she was probably at the courthouse swearing out a restraining order. He wouldn't fight it, but he would make sure she never needed it.

Paul hung his head in the close, stifling room. Right now he hated Fletcher Streiker more than anything. Streiker knew that this resolution was necessary for Paul and Royce both, so he set Paul on a cliff and told him to step forward. It was necessary, and it hurt more than anything—more than losing Kris, more than losing his ministry. It was the third strike.

He sat thinking, *What now? Get a job, go to work, come home, go to bed, get up, go to work? Why?* After demonstrating himself incapable of maintaining any meaningful occupation or relationship, what was the point of doing anything? In detachment, he looked down at the black hole of oblivion gaping at his feet. Interesting how there was no sadness. Was this what it felt like to die?—in the grip of pain, and death, was it a mercy that the heart died first?

His phone warbled, which startled him so that he almost slipped off the hard bed frame. Collecting himself, he pulled out his phone and looked at the display: unknown name, and a number he didn't recognize. His first thought, ironically, was that Worldwide Delivery had found some reason to disqualify his application. "Hello?"

A voice he didn't recognize mumbled something. He pressed the phone to his ear. "Excuse me?" It was such an irritant when people ate, or drank, or blew their noses while on the phone.

"Sorry," the voice said, clearer. "It's Royce."

9

"Royce?" Paul gasped, his heart palpitating. Immediately he was disbelieving. "Royce?" he repeated skeptically. *Buddy, if this is your idea of a joke, I'm going to—*

"Yeah, I—achoo! Sorry, I'b just—achoo! Ah choo! Oh, I got this terr'bul code—I feel like I'b dying—ah CHOO!"

At first he was speechless. "I could bring you some soup," he whispered.

She seemed not to hear him. There was a rustle, then she said, "I got your bessages (sniffle). I'b sorry about Walt. What—ah choo!—happened?"

"He had a heart attack. It was all quick and painless, as far as the doctor knew," he said.

"I'b really sorry. Doesn't Jeannine need you?" she asked. Then he heard her sneeze resoundingly away from the phone.

"No. She's fine," he said intently. "Royce, can I see you?"

"Oh, no. AHH-CHOO. I'b not letting anybody see be like this."

"But don't you need medicine? Let me bring you something," he pleaded.

"I'b all doped up, and I jus' need sobe sleep. Lebbe call you later, okay? Ah choo!"

"All right," he said unwillingly. *I love you; I love you,* he ached to add, but she had hung up.

In total shock, he closed the phone. Then he got up and left that old shack forever.

Too distracted to do anything useful—such as apply for work at any of the other companies he had selected— he just drove around some more. But when other drivers started honking at him again, he knew he needed to stop somewhere. So he pulled into a little café that was jammed with lunchtime patrons. But since nobody wanted to sit outside on the patio, he was able to get a seat immediately at a shaded, isolated table.

He got ice water, chips and salsa to keep him occupied until the kitchen could produce a side order of enchiladas for him—not a full meal. He felt like he'd done nothing but eat lately.

Waiting, he propped his elbows on the table to absently break chips. An attentive sparrow alighted on the chair opposite him, cocking its head. He flipped a chip fragment to the concrete beneath the chair, and the sparrow flapped down to snatch it up. Other sparrows converged to fight over the prize, which the original claimant lost. Paul tossed another crumb to him, but this a crow made off with.

So Paul dropped a crumb directly at his feet. The birds eyed it, but only the first sparrow was bold enough to come get it. He landed six inches from Paul's feet to eat the tiny piece, then looked up at him expectantly.

Paul dropped another; this one the sparrow picked up and carried off.

At least she's speaking to me. But that, in itself, did not guarantee a reconciliation. Some penance would be required of him, possibly some proof of his intentions. His hands itched for his phone, to call her right back and make all kinds of promises about putting her needs first —which was enormously ironic, considering that what she needed was to sleep off this cold, and if he insisted on calling her, she'd quickly regret having any pity on him whatsoever.

He sat back for the waitress to place a small plate of enchiladas before him and refill his water, then he began mechanically eating. He wasn't all that hungry, but, growing up as poor as he did, he could not bring himself to waste food, and cleaned the plate.

Sipping the water, he leaned back to look over the hedge of yaupon (practically indestructible) to the traffic just past it. He was a little surprised that Royce would stay in Texas—but then again, she said she liked the sunshine. As long as she could have the comfort of a bustling civilization close by (meaning stores, coffee shops, and art museums) then, apparently, she was okay.

Couldn't he do better for her than a delivery job? For pete's sake, he had a master's degree. At that point, inspiration settled upon his befuddled brain like the dew: Why shouldn't he apply to The Streiker Corporation? It was a big company. If Royce was unwilling to take him back, or even see him, he wasn't running the risk of stalking her by applying there, especially since he knew not to apply to the bookstore.

He was tentatively feeling out the idea when the

waitress suddenly slapped his lunch tab on the table. She was harried with too many tables, impatient with having to run out in the heat to wait on one customer who ordered water and a side dish.

So he stood, producing a twenty to cover the bill and an extremely generous tip. While she, misunderstanding, took the twenty in exasperation to go get change, he paused to dump the rest of the chips on the ground for the birds, and went back out to his truck. With the engine idling and the air conditioning running, he pulled out his phone to mull over the numbers.

The main headquarters of The Streiker Corporation was in Dallas, and he did not wish to drive clear out there—not when Royce was here. He had the personal assistant's number (her name was . . . ?) but he was leery of abusing it. And he sure wasn't going to call the head honcho to pull strings for him. How pathetic would that be? But there was another option.

He leaned down to sift through his papers on the floorboard, coming up with the list of Streiker-owned companies in Fort Worth. Though he perused these twelve intently, it wasn't apparent from a company name and address what the function of each might be. Feeling that it was ill-advised to apply to a company without knowing anything about it, Paul folded the sheet, put the truck in gear, and drove back to the public library downtown. Taking his list inside, he sat back down at one of the computers to research the Streiker companies.

He crossed the bookstore and the art gallery off his list immediately. Number three was a printer/distributor that specialized in reissuing out-of-print classics such as *The Aeneid* that he had bought (and realized for the first time that he'd left in the store). That was a possibility. He had no experience in printing, but he was a good reader.

Number seven was a classic car shop, specializing in the restoration and servicing of vintage vehicles. As Paul clicked through photos of restored beauties—a 1955 Hudson Hornet, a 1933 Plymouth 5-window coupe, a 1963 Chevy II Nova 2-door convertible—he felt the tug of the little boy for all things shiny and mechanical. He put an asterisk beside that entry, despite the fact that he knew little about cars beyond routine maintenance. But by now, he was getting a feel for the areas that interested Streiker, at least in Fort Worth: restoring old houses, old books and old thought; restoring rusted, abandoned vehicles; restoring useless people.

Paul extracted a couple other possibilities from the list, particularly a horticulturalist who made a pointed plea on his website for bilingual job-seekers. Being hypersensitive about his background, Paul finally rejected that option on some flimsy pretext.

Then, as he looked at his findings objectively, he conceded that most of these jobs required a specialized skill or training that he lacked. There was little likelihood of his walking off the street into a position with any of them.

Then there was Number Eleven: Officina Gentium. Wasn't that Latin? It rang a faint bell. But Paul couldn't find anything on it other than an address. This he located on an internet map, and found it to be in an old warehouse district (of course) on the Trinity River.

Dubiously, he got up from the computer to solicit a librarian's help. Showing her the entry, he explained that he was interested in applying to work for this company, but didn't have a clue what they did.

She took the paper and peered at his handwriting through her bifocals. "Officina Gentium. That is Latin for 'workshop of the world,'" she observed.

"Interesting," he agreed. "I couldn't find a webpage or any web information on them. Is there some resource I'm overlooking?"

"Let's see," she said, and led him to a shelf full of indexes.

Over the next hour, they both looked, and came up with nothing other than the original listing in *Hoover's Handbook* that gave it as a Streiker-owned company, with the address. "This is highly unusual. But then, it may have gone out of business," she noted.

"Probably," he agreed. "Well, thanks anyway."

"You're welcome."

Returning to his truck, he sat behind the wheel to assess his progress over the last two and a half hours. As he went over the list that he had memorized by now, his eye kept going back to number eleven. Well, since Royce hadn't called him back yet, and the rest of his day appeared relatively free. . . . He exited the library parking lot toward the warehouse district.

Officina Gentium, he mused. Then he remembered where he'd run across that before: in one of his peripheral college readings. It was part of a larger statement—what was it? *officina gentium, vagina nationum*: "the source of races, the mother of nations," as an ancient historian said of the homeland of the Scandinavians. Over time, the meaning of the phrase had apparently altered according to evolving use. And now, here, it meant something that Streiker was doing. Or had been doing, if the company no longer existed.

After meandering up and down streets with no clear addresses, Paul located the correct building via the six-inch-high numerals, faded but legible, painted on the brick. He parked across the street and emerged from his truck in disappointment. The old warehouse certainly looked deserted—no cars, no activity. Other than a few loading hands working at an adjacent warehouse, Paul saw no one. He surveyed the two-story brick building; its second-floor windows with turn-of-the-century ornamentation gazed back at him like sightless eyes.

Hesitantly, he went up to a street-level wooden door with peeling paint. He knocked on the door, leaning forward to listen. When he didn't hear anything in reply —as he expected not to—he put his hand to the rusted doorknob and turned. Pushing proved fruitless, and he had almost concluded that the door was barred on the inside before he accidentally discovered that it opened outward. The hinges were just invisible.

Paul stepped into a vacant, echoing interior with concrete floor and brick walls. He looked up at the high windows, which allowed some light to filter in through the grime. Whatever second floor there had been was now gone; from the front door he could see clear to the slatted ceiling, crisscrossed by exposed ductwork. Rows of round industrial lights, presently off, ran from the front of the building to the back. The cavernous space, which Paul guessed to be about 45,000 square feet, was empty but for a 1940's office desk and chair in the middle of the floor.

After noting the furniture, he continued to scan the

warehouse. Old electric wiring lay exposed along the wall, running from the old-fashioned light button beside the door to the central row of lighting fixtures hanging from the ceiling forty feet over his head.

Experimentally, Paul pushed the button and looked up: one row of lights, the center row, came on one at a time, beginning with the light above the door. They cast bright circles on the concrete floor, catching the desk and chair in the center light, then progressing to the rear of the warehouse. This enabled him to see that there was nothing in the whole place but the desk and chair. And something on the desk.

Placed so conspicuously in the center of the warehouse, the desk invited attention, so Paul walked over to investigate. Halfway there, he stopped abruptly and looked up at the sound of whooshing air. Though he did not feel anything, he saw air vents high in the walls, as well as along the floor. Then he realized that it was comfortable in here, certainly not warmer than 75 degrees. But—he canvassed the closed windows—it should have been broiling. Since it wasn't, he had to assume that the warehouse was air-conditioned.

Paul absorbed that thought for a moment, then resumed his walk to the desk. There was a sheet of paper with a sticky note on it. Coming around to the chair side of the desk to look at the paper right side up, he was shaken to see written on the sticky note, "For Paul Arrendondo." He removed the note to look at the paper. It was a printed employment application for Officina Gentium.

Suddenly weak, Paul sank into the chair. He scanned the form blankly for a minute, until he could collect his senses to read coherently. It appeared to be one of those essay-type applications—few questions and large spaces for reply. It was only one page. Slowly, he drew his pen from his pocket and began to place the tip in the first blank. Then he saw a hand-drawn arrow pointing to a line in the instructions that said, "Use black ink." Scrawled next to this was the handwritten prohibitive: "Not blue!"

Paul stared at the pen that he had taken from his pocket. Yes, it was blue ink. How did they know . . . ? He laid the form back down and looked over the clean desk. Then he opened the top drawer to find a—that is, one—black pen. He took it from the drawer with shaking fingers and read over the brief instructions thoroughly: "Answer the questions asked as completely as possible. Print. Use black ink." Only then did he begin to fill out the application.

First blank: "Full name." So he printed (as per instructions), "Paul Robert Arrendondo." Beside that was: "Phone number." He wrote that down.

Second blank: "Date wife left." "Wha—?" he muttered. Nervously, he wrote, "About a month ago." Too late, his eye was drawn back to the first word, *Date.* "Dang," he muttered. The form asked for the *date* Royce had left.

He put the pen down again and looked in every drawer for a spare application, but the desk was empty. He had to make do with this form. So he squeezed the additional explanation in the space provided, "Approx. July 15." The follow-up question to that was: "Can you be more specific?" "No," he wrote.

Third blank: "Date father died." This he knew; it

was just last Friday. Today was Monday, the fourteenth. Counting back the days on his fingers, he printed the correct date. The follow-up asked, "Where is your mother?" "At the Ferring ranch outside San Angelo, TX" he wrote, without the least doubt that they already knew where the Ferring ranch was. But at least he felt that he was answering the questions correctly. He dimly noted that they seemed more interested in his personal relationships than his work history.

Fourth blank: "Why do you want to work for Officina Gentium?"

This he thought about for a long time. It was a hard question to answer, since he didn't know what the company did, or what job he was applying for. All he knew about the company was who owned it.

So he wrote, "Mr. Streiker has been very helpful to me. I would like to repay him in some small way." He paused, thinking that *small* smacked of false humility. But, seriously, how much help could he offer a multi-billionaire? The follow-up question was, "Is that the only reason?"

He exhaled, "This is the first interactive paper application I've ever filled out!" But then he wrote, "I want to have a good job for Royce, to give her a reason to give me another chance." It was not a beautiful sentence, but he didn't try to change it.

Fifth blank: "What are you willing to do?"

He twirled the pen, thinking, then wrote, "I will do whatever Mr. Streiker wants me to do."

The follow-up asked, "Really?"

"Argh!" He put his head in his hands. But then it dawned on him that it was a legitimate question. What if

Streiker wanted him in, say, Dallas? Chicago? Nigeria? What if he had to choose between the job and Royce?

Paul studied the pen, thinking. There was no question in his mind that Streiker had enabled him to find Royce. But what if, after all that, she declined to take him back? Or what if he discovered—and here he wilted—that having her was *not* the deepest desire of his heart?

He inhaled, sinking back into the chair. How could he know what was most important to him until he knew what the job entailed? Or until he knew what Royce wanted? With this question, the whole issue seemed to rotate until he felt as if he was looking at it upside down —he even leaned a little to try to keep his balance.

Then he realized that the question had been righted for him to its proper position: the whole decision hinged on Royce, not him. Pursuing her as if she were an object would gain him nothing, because the concept was a mirage. If he wanted Royce to have him, he had to make himself worthy of having. Now, could working for Streiker accomplish that?

Paul leaned forward to write, "YES."

And that was it. That was the last question. Paul flipped the paper over, but the back was blank. They hadn't even asked for his address, work history, or Social Security number. Then he reasoned that if they knew what color pen he was using, they probably knew those details, as well.

Somewhat disconcerted, he stood, laying the pen atop the application on the desk. He glanced around for a drop box, or something, but the warehouse space was otherwise emphatically empty. He stepped away from the desk, pushing in the chair as if he needed to keep a walkway clear, and headed for the door.

He paused, reconsidering: should he take the application with him? He snorted in reply, "What am I going to do with it?" Besides, no instructions had been left to that effect. No; he found it here, so it needed to stay here. Obviously, someone would come by to pick it up.

Emerging from the cool warehouse into the hot afternoon, Paul paused to put on his sunglasses. How did they know he would come here? He climbed into his truck, turning the ignition and flipping the air on *high*. And what if he hadn't followed through so diligently on the leads he had uncovered? Glancing over his shoulder, he pulled away from the curb. Well, for better or ill, he'd done all he could there. The next move was theirs.

He pulled out into 5 o'clock traffic, restlessly tapping the wheel. It had been—what?—six hours since he had talked to Royce? Wasn't that enough time for her to rest? But, she said she'd call. He mustn't stalk. Well, yeah, but persevering was not stalking—she hadn't told him *not* to call. He just needed a good reason.

Paul's attention seized on a corner deli coming up. He cut across two lanes of traffic, eliciting angry honks, to pull up to its front. It was not too crowded yet. Seeing as they had the marketing savvy to post a menu in the window, Paul climbed out of his truck to stand under the striped green awning and glance through the menu. He pulled out his phone, scrolled to a recent number, and dialed.

After the third ring, there was a mumbled answer: "Uhm-huh."

"Hi. How are you feeling? You sound a lot better," Paul said.

A long sigh. "I stopped sneezing. 'At's about all."

"You really need to eat to get better. I'm at Corner Bakery now, looking at their menu. They've got soups—ah, there's minestrone, cheddar broccoli, roasted tomato. They've got Santa Fe ranch salad, Caesar salad with chicken, the chopped salad with chicken, bacon, avocado, and bleu cheese. If you feel up to a sandwich, they've got chicken pasta, turkey, ham, roast beef, tuna. They've also got panini and pasta. So what sounds good?"

There was a long pause while Paul chewed his lip. "What kind of pasta?" she asked.

He quickly looked back to the menu, to read off the choices to her. She then confessed, "The Pesto Cavatappi sounds good."

"Do you want a Caesar salad or mixed greens with that?" he asked.

"Caesar."

"Okay. Iced tea or soft drink?"

"Iced tea," she said.

"Okay, then, great." He took a breath. "Where do I bring it, Royce?"

She didn't hesitate quite as long this time. "Um, the Cypress Garden apartments on Eighth," she said. "Number one twenty-four."

"I know where that is. I'll be right there with dinner," he said quietly.

"Thanks, Paul," she murmured.

Hurrying inside, he ordered her choices, a sandwich meal for himself, two brownies, and drinks, to go. It set him back another twenty dollars, but he emerged from the deli with stuffed white sacks and a hopeful heart.

He did begrudge the heavy traffic, which turned a fifteen-minute drive into thirty. For most of the way he was riding the bumper of the driver in front of him, who was unfortunate enough to be trapped between two males in pickups.

But soon enough Paul was pulling up to the modest apartment complex, scanning the building for numbers. He found her unit, but had to park some distance from it, in visitor parking. (He knew how ready these apartments were to enforce towing.) Then he practically ran to her door, sloshing a little tea from under an insecure lid.

Taking a deep breath, he stood at number 124 while he transferred both sacks and drinks to one arm to ring the doorbell.

10

Arms full, Paul watched as the door was opened a crack around a chain. He glimpsed hazel eyes under mussed hair—the door was shut again; the chain removed, then the door opened wide. Paul gazed at Royce standing in a long sports shirt, legs bare. But what sent shock waves through him was the short, layered cut with bangs that lay tousled around her face. Royce had always been fiercely proud of her long hair, and spent a lot of time grooming it. From the looks of it, she'd cut off about ten inches.

"Come in," she murmured, as he still stood on the threshold.

"Thanks." He snapped out of his daze long enough to bring in dinner, glancing around the small apartment. The front room was about the size of his closet at the York; the only furniture it held was a table with a decent computer set-up, and a chair.

"In the kitchen," Royce directed, so he took the sacks to a tea table with two chairs next to a double window off the box-sized kitchen. She sank into one chair, daubing at a red nose, while Paul unloaded the food and placed it before her. "Thanks so much," she mumbled. "I hope you got something for yourself."

"I never forget myself," he said, taking his sandwich out of the bag. He sat tentatively, watching as she opened the plastic container of pasta and unwrapped a plastic fork. "You look good," he said quietly.

She glanced up wryly. "You get Diplomat of the Year Award. I'm too vain to call you a liar. Bet that was a shock, to see my hair gone." She took a large bite of pasta.

He shrugged, "Everybody needs a change now and then." Absently, he began unwrapping his sandwich.

"So what happened with Walt?" she asked.

"He . . . we were out in the lower pasture and he just dropped. By the time I called nine-one-one and got him back to the house, he was dead. Doctor said he thought it was pretty much instantaneous." Remembering what he was doing, he began unwrapping paper again.

"I'm really sorry, Paul. Did you get hold of Buddy?" She looked up over her tea.

"Yeah, finally." He had to look away from her eyes so that he wouldn't reach over the table and wrap his arms around her. "He and Renetta were in, uh, the Caribbean, where the reception was lousy. But they got to the ranch before I left."

"They're always jetting all over the place. I hate that they do that," she grumbled.

"Me, too," he murmured, drooping.

"It's not fair," she pouted around a mouthful.

"No," he said.

She stopped eating to study him. "Why did you leave the ranch?"

"Royce, I—" he flailed a little. "I wanted to get you back! I've been kicking myself that things got so bad between us—I never should have let it get to that point. I —tried to call you, but when you wouldn't pick up—" He aborted the sentence. The last thing he wanted to do was start blaming her.

She groaned, "I lost my phone right after I got into town. Can you believe it? I think somebody swiped it!" She took another bite. "This is really good. Anyway, when I got another phone I tried to call, but got cut off."

"I—don't know what happened with that, Royce. Renetta told me just a couple days ago that Shana told her that you called—I didn't even know that you had tried to call, or I sure would've—"

"It's okay, Paul," she said mildly. "Eat your sandwich. I'd feel better."

Dutifully, he took a bite, and they ate in silence for a while. The small table had a glass top, so that he couldn't help looking at her legs . . . smooth, tanned . . . pink toenails. Breathing harder, he looked up—straight into the bedroom behind her. There were two twin beds. *That's okay, I don't need much space. We can always hit the floor.* The implication of two beds did not sink into his befuddled brain right away. He lowered his eyes again, trying to just eat and not think and especially not look at her.

She then asked, "How did you find me?"

He tried to think of the best spin to put on it, but all he could get out were the bare facts: "Ah, Renetta called your dad, and he told her you'd called from Fort Worth. So I came on up here, and ran into Fletcher Streiker. He told me you were still in town. So I . . . began hitting places I thought you might've been to—the Phoenix Street Center, first. The new director, Mitch, told me you'd been by looking for the other centers, or something. So I went to Gold Cord, and found your interview sheet; found that you applied to The Streiker Corporation, found the Streiker companies in Fort Worth, then just . . . asked everywhere," he finished lamely.

"Can I ask you something?" he blurted. Without waiting for an answer, he went on, "How did you get from Fort Worth to Gold Cord in Dallas and back to Fort Worth? Are you driving? Got a car?"

She closed her mouth in an ironic smile, stirring her pasta. "No and no. I never went to Dallas. They interviewed me over the phone."

"Oh," he said. That simple explanation had never occurred to him.

Then she observed, "You did a lot of legwork."

His eyes started watering, and he put down the sandwich. "I really want to try again, Royce. I really want you back. I've—applied to work at a Streiker company here in town. It's called, uh"—his mind was a blank—"Officina Gentium."

She said nothing, only blinked. He dropped his hands in his lap because he didn't trust them. "You don't have to give me an answer right away. I'm not gonna push you. I'm staying at the, ah, York Bed and Breakfast till I hear something from the O. G., but, I want you to feel like you can call me if you need anything. I carry my phone with me everywhere. I sleep with it," he rambled.

"Oh, Paul." She reached toward his face and that

was all the permission he needed. He lunged over the table to grab her shoulders and plant his mouth on hers. "Umph—Paul, I'll make you sick!" she protested, turning her head.

"I hope so," he breathed, lifting her. He pressed her up against the wall beside the window. "Please, please make me just as sick as you are. Let me spend all day in bed with you, sick as a dog."

"Paul!" she gasped, half laughing. But she twined her arms around his neck.

He had lowered one hand to fumble with his belt and unzip his jeans when they heard a key turning in the door lock. Royce quickly slid out from between him and the wall and sat at the table.

"That's my roommate," she murmured, picking up her fork.

Paul rezipped his pants, sitting and breathing. The sudden fear rose in him that her roommate was a man— how could she do this to him? They were still married! Paul looked toward the door in wrath and apprehension of what he was about to do. He didn't want to go to jail for beating in the legal resident's head. That would not help his case with Royce.

He saw at a glance the hair, dress, and high heels of the person entering, and his anger morphed into shame at his lack of faith in his wife. When the woman looked up and saw them, recognition passed between him and her.

Royce turned from the table. "Hi, Miriam. This is my husband, Paul. He brought me some get-well food."

"Yes, we met. He came to the gallery yesterday," she said, evaluating him.

"Hi," he nodded awkwardly.

"Oh, yes. That's right. You left a message on my phone," Royce said.

Paul stood, gathering his half-eaten sandwich in the paper. "I won't impose any more on you today. Just . . ." he struggled, "call me if you need anything."

"Okay. Thanks again," Royce said.

Leaving everything else on the table, he passed Miriam in the tiny front room, muttering, "Bye."

She watched him leave, then came to stand over the tea table. "Can I have a brownie?"

Royce grinned, gesturing to it.

Somehow, Paul made it back to the York. He purchased a soft drink from the dinner buffet and took it upstairs to the Baron's Closet. First thing, he noticed that his room had been straightened, bed made, and washstand equipped with fresh water and towel. Also, his clean, pressed clothes were hanging in a plastic bag on the back of the door.

Paul transferred them to the wardrobe, then sat on the bed to finish the sandwich. Since so much was riding on a telephone call from several parties, he dug through a suitcase for his phone charger and plugged it in. Settling back on the bed, he stared at the wall.

He had found Royce; she was speaking to him. He should have been grateful, but he wasn't—he was peeved, irritated, and above all, frustrated. He had been definitely banking on an instant resolution one way or another—that once he found her, she would either come back to him or tell him to get lost. But all that happened was that he brought her dinner and had enough contact to almost lose his mind and physically assault the next person who walked in the door.

He had to be patient; he knew that. He had to let her decide what she wanted. But knowing and doing were two different animals, and he didn't know if he could—

A realization washed over him like cold water: this was part of that desire Streiker talked about. Certain personality types were willing to do anything to accomplish their goals, except wait. Waiting was the hardest test of all. When you had done all you could, and the direction of your life lay in someone else's power, were you willing to sit back and allow the natural outcome of your choices to manifest itself? It could be distasteful—even bitter. But it was the only way to avoid self-delusion.

Vaguely wishing that he had gone by the bookstore to retrieve his copy of *The Aeneid*, Paul turned out the lights early that night. He was exhausted.

By the time he awakened the following morning, he was too late to get first use of the bathroom, and had to stand in line. When he finally got his turn, he discovered a wet, disorderly mess, no hot water, and not a clean towel in sight. So he took a sixty-second, shivering shower, then had to dry himself with the least wet towel from the floor.

After dressing, he found himself downstairs minutes after the breakfast buffet had closed, so he had to settle for fast-food coffee and biscuits. Then came the hard part: deciding what to do with himself all day.

He studied his watch far longer than he needed to in order to determine what time it was. In fact, if the Old Book Shoppe opened at ten o'clock, it would have opened twenty minutes ago. So, he could go pick up his book. And, if Royce was there, he could just . . . say hello. He was determined not to follow her around like a puppy.

So he proceeded downtown to the bookstore. The day was a scorcher, as is normal for Texas in August; the temperature had probably hit 100 an hour ago. The interior of his truck was just beginning to cool off by the time Paul pulled up to the bookstore. Advancing to the front door, he took off his sunglasses to note the hours of operation: Monday through Friday, 9:30 to 6:30; Saturday, 9 to 8; Sunday, 1 to 5. He went on inside, relaxing in the quiet coolness.

He went directly to the counter—the clerk there might have been the same one he bought the book from, but he hadn't paid much attention to her, so couldn't remember. When she looked up, he said, "Hi. My name is Paul Arrendondo—I bought a copy of *The Aeneid* yesterday, and must have left it—"

"Yeah." She reached under the counter to bring up the book with a sticky note on the cover. She discarded the note theoretically before he could see that it said, "Bought by dummy who left w/out it." "Here you go."

"Thanks." He took possession of his property, then paused. "I don't suppose Royce felt well enough to make it in today."

The girl glanced at a contraption perched on a shelf on the side wall. It looked like an amalgamation of exploding parts from a 1920's kitchen, but there must have been a clock face in there somewhere, because she said, "She got a late start this morning, but Miriam's bringing her in about fifteen minutes, if you want to wait."

"Yeah, sure. I wanted to start reading this, anyway."

He went over to a reading niche within sight of the front door, made himself comfortable, and began reading.

Despite the fact that this was a superior translation to the one he'd started years ago, he found himself reading the same lines over and over again. He would read a few lines, glance up at the front door, lose his place, and start over. Then again, while his eyes were dutifully focused on the page, his thoughts were running: *So Miriam brings her to work. That makes sense, with the art gallery just a few blocks away. What do they do if Royce needs to go in and Miriam can't drive her? Maybe I can help.*

Book open on his lap, he was soon reduced to staring at the front door. Then his phone warbled with a suddenness that made the book somersault out of his hands. Picking it up and extracting the phone from his pocket at the same time, he looked at the number display. It wasn't Buddy's or Royce's. So he answered, "Hello?"

"Hello, Paul. This is Vince Harrison, president of Officina Gentium. Would you like to come in for an interview?"

"Uh, sure. Yes," Paul said, surprised.

"All right. See you in ten minutes." And he hung up.

Paul stared at his phone. "Ten minutes!" He got up to return to the counter. When the clerk looked up, he said, "I—just got a call for a job interview, so I'll see Royce a little later."

"Sure," she said, with an expression of, *Do I care?*

Disconcerted, he put on his sunglasses and went back out to his truck, tossing the book on the floorboard (cleaner than the still-stained seat). As he left the parking lot, he glanced around for Miriam and Royce, but didn't see them. Then he braked. "Interview *where*?" The warehouse. Had to be. He just wasn't sure he could make it in ten minutes.

He got his bearings, then turned the wheel toward the warehouse district. He fretted over the fact that he wasn't dressed for an interview—jeans, boots, and cotton shirt—but apparently that didn't matter. He also felt slightly uneasy that they were apparently monitoring his movements—else how would Mr. Harrison know he was only ten minutes away? If he hustled.

Exactly ten minutes later, Paul was pulling up to the old warehouse. He hurried to the same painted door and opened it without preface. Inside, it was all just as before, except that a man sat behind the desk, and a second chair sat in front of it.

Paul advanced, his boots loud on the concrete floor, and reached out a hand over the desk. "Mr. Harrison? I'm Paul Arrendondo."

"Hello, Paul." The fellow—early forties, nicely groomed, casually dressed—shook his hand, then gestured, "Have a seat." When Paul did, Harrison noted, "You made it in eleven minutes."

"You didn't give me much time," Paul observed, shifting in the hard wooden seat.

Harrison smiled. "Sorry. The truth is, I would have waited no matter how long it took you to get here. It's just a point of interest to see how someone responds to an unreasonable demand."

Paul blinked. "You didn't know where I was?"

The president studied him. "How would I know where you were?"

Paul shrugged, "I guess you wouldn't, but, I just happened to be ten minutes away, at the Old Book Shoppe. I would have been here right on time had I not stopped to tell the clerk that I was leaving for a job interview."

"Ah. Good point. The first thing you need to learn is not to explain what you're doing. It's a waste of time," Harrison explained.

Paul snorted. "Literally. She couldn't have cared less."

Harrison nodded. "What were you doing at the Old Book Shoppe?"

"Well, I—accidentally left a book there I'd bought yesterday—*The Aeneid*."

He hesitated preparatory to explaining that he'd also been hoping to see Royce, and Harrison asked, "What about *The Aeneid* interested you?"

"Well, I just got sucked into the story, I guess." Paul gulped at the unexpected question. "About fifteen years ago I read *The Iliad* and *The Odyssey* for a college class, so the following summer I picked up *The Aeneid*, and . . . here's Aeneas running from defeat at Troy; although he has divine parentage, he's real; he's vulnerable. But because of his—his honor and sense of duty to his father and his mission, he achieves his destiny in founding Rome. He gains the golden bough to enter the underworld because he's called by fate, and he wins his battles because he submits to the greater will of the gods—"

Pierced by the irony of it, Paul looked at his interviewer. "What happens when duty and destiny don't match up so neatly?—when being a faithful son and pastor gets you nothing but crapped on? *Literally*."

Harrison's steady gaze shamed Paul into looking away. *What am I thinking, bringing up all that?* But then Harrison said, "If you hadn't been through everything with your parents, your first marriage, your failed pastorate, the Ferrings, and Royce, we wouldn't be able to use you."

Paul squinted at him. "How so? I don't understand." *Shee, how much about me do they* know*, already?*

"The only question now," Harrison went on, leaning back, "is whether you've learned anything or just gotten brittle."

Paul stared at him, feeling his heart flailing around in his ribcage. "I want to learn. I just don't know what to do."

"Okay," Harrison said.

Paul's phone warbled, causing him to start up. "I'm sorry—I should've turned it off," he said, groping to do so.

"Go ahead and answer it," Harrison nodded.

Reluctantly, Paul put it to his ear. "Hello?"

"Oh—hi, Paul." It was Royce. "I hope I'm not bothering you. I have a favor to ask—Miriam was supposed to take me into work, but her battery is dead. Could you possibly come get me?"

"I—I would, Royce, but—"

"We're done here," Harrison said.

Paul stared at him briefly, then said into the phone, "Okay, yeah, I'll be right there."

"Thanks so much," she said.

He closed his phone, standing. "What . . . happens now?"

"We'll be in touch," Harrison nodded.

"Okay. Thank you." Paul again reached over to shake his hand, then walked out to his truck in the blazing sunshine. He flipped the air conditioner to *high* as he turned the wheel toward Eighth Street. *How bizarre a job interview was that? How did they know about my pastorate and Kris—my whole life? How badly did I come off there? "We'll be in touch"? Is that a kiss-off?*

Arriving at Royce's apartment slightly flustered and sweaty, he rang the doorbell and waited. A minute later she emerged, turning to lock the door behind her. Paul regarded her short skirt and long legs. "You look nice. Feeling better?"

"Well enough," she sighed, smiling faintly. "Thanks so much, Paul."

He glanced around. "Where's Miriam? Maybe I can jump start her car. I've got cables."

Royce shook her head. "She had it jumped twice last week. It's just kaput. Oh, my, you still driving that old truck?" she laughed.

"Why would I drive anything else?" he asked. "Well, go tell her I'll take her to get a new battery, after I drop you off."

Royce turned serious eyes on him. "She's not here. Her brother came to pick her up and take her to the hospital—their mom has been in the cardiac care unit for a week, and it doesn't look good."

"I'm sorry," he said.

"Yeah." She opened the door to climb into the cab, then paused, eyes widening. Settling into the seat, she gingerly avoided the faded brown spot. And she tried not to step on the papers and book on the floor.

Paul slid behind the wheel. With a troubled expression, he turned the ignition. "Well, when is she getting back? She's going to have to do something to get your transportation up and running."

"No kidding." Royce hesitated. "She's probably going to be there all night, if her mom lasts that long. She's just not able to do anything about it today. But . . . if you could . . . replace her battery, I'm sure she'd pay you for it."

Paul glanced at her as he turned a corner. "I'd need her keys."

Royce immediately opened her purse and handed him a loose key. "There."

He nodded vaguely, dropping the key into his shirt pocket as he pulled up to The Old Book Shoppe. "Yeah, I'll—what kind of car does she have?"

"Oh, yeah, you'd need to know that," she laughed. "It's the white Ford right next to the door."

"Okay. Um, how about a radio code? Alarm system?" he asked.

She looked blank, then said, "Paul, it's a ninety-nine. There's nothing fancy on it."

"Okay," he acknowledged. As she opened the door to get out, he added, "Royce, I'm going to need to get into your apartment to wash up afterwards, particularly if I get any battery acid on me."

Did she actually hesitate? "Sure." She opened her purse again and fished out her key ring to give to him. "The apartment key's the big one, obviously. Can you pick me up at 6:30, since you have my keys?"

"Sure," he said.

"Okay. Thanks so much." She flashed her smile at him, the one that set his pulse racing, then closed the cab door and hurried into the store.

Mulling over this turn of events, Paul drove back to the Cypress Gardens apartments, parking next to the old white Ford. He walked around it, noting the worn tires and lackluster finish. Unlocking it, he sat behind the wheel and turned the ignition: *click-click-click*. He flipped on the windshield wipers, watching them creep up a few inches before stopping altogether. That pretty well told him what he needed to know.

He let himself into the apartment, rigidly avoiding the bedroom, and gently ransacked the kitchen for baking soda, which he dissolved in a plastic bowl of water (to neutralize any spilled battery acid). This, with a roll of paper towels, he took back outside to the disabled car. Retrieving his tool box from the truck, he popped the hood, rolled up his sleeves, and set to work removing the old battery.

He put it in the bed of his pickup—the store that sold him a new battery would be happy to dispose of this one for him. Before going shopping, he went back inside the apartment to use the bathroom and wash his hands. Since he didn't see anything in the tiny bathroom that indicated a male presence, he successfully resisted the temptation to snoop.

However, he did succumb to the computer on the way out. Moving the mouse brought up an e-mail account for Miriam. (This was obviously her computer, as Royce didn't leave the ranch with one and didn't leave with enough money to buy one.) Paul wasn't even tempted to read any of Miriam's mail (most of which was from a "Doctor Bear") but he did click on Favorites, just to see if Royce might have anything up. The top favorite sites were local news, fashions, and celebrity gossip. Paul closed the browser window and went on out.

Careful to lock up the apartment and the car, he took the battery to the first auto parts store he could find. To his gratification, they were running a sale, so Paul was able to get a new, higher-rated battery than the old one for a mere sixty bucks. The bad news was that his second credit card, the American Express that he thought he had a little leeway on, was rejected, so he had to pay cash. But for Royce, it was worth it.

He drove through a burger joint to get a very late lunch, then returned to the apartments to install Miriam's new battery. That done, he washed up again and sat behind the sedan's wheel to try the ignition. The engine turned over at once; Paul listened to the rough idling for a minute, noting that it needed a tune-up. Resolutely, he turned the ignition back off. If this were Royce's car—and he had the money—he'd take it to a shop, a tire store, and a car wash; but he wasn't going to start taking care of Miriam, too.

By then, it was after six, so he drove on down to The Old Book Shoppe to pick up Royce, arriving with about ten minutes to spare. He could have gone inside to wait, where it was more comfortable, but he parked in the shade and rolled down both windows.

About twenty minutes later, she emerged with the other girl he'd bought the book from. Royce stopped to look around; he waved and she hurried over. As he watched her swing toward him, he considered that

Miriam would probably be up at the hospital all night long.

He opened the passenger door from where he sat for Royce to bounce in. "Oh! Paul, what is that awful smell? What happened?" She scrunched away from the stain.

"An accident. Long story. Sorry," he said, starting the engine and the air conditioner. He didn't want to burden her with the depressing story of his father's death right now. Maybe later, after a good bonding session.

"Were you able to do anything for Miriam's poor car?" she asked.

"Yeah, got her a battery. Oh, yeah. Here." He stopped in the parking lot to give her all the keys, plus the receipt. "It was on sale."

"Great! Thanks so much. She'll appreciate it so much," Royce said, perusing the receipt before putting it in her purse.

Sitting on the brake in the parking lot, he asked, "Want do you want for dinner? Remember the Chinese food place on Camp Bowie?"

She looked slightly perturbed. "Yes. It was okay. Paul, I don't want you to buy me dinner again."

"Why not? You have to eat; I have to eat," he said. Still she hesitated, and he nodded, "La Hacienda is right here, and I can see they're not very crowded."

She smiled at him fleetingly. "Sure. Why not."

So he crossed over two parking lots. They went in and got a table right away; when they ordered, Royce selected the cheapest entrée on the dinner menu, and water to drink.

Paul eyed her. "Water? What's wrong with tea? If you're gonna start changing beverages on me, go to a margarita." She laughed, but declined to alter her order.

Silence hung heavy over their table while they waited for their food. Paul asked, "How are you feeling?"

"A lot better," she said, glancing up. "Just a little headache."

"Was the store busy?"

"Not really. We get most of our business on the weekends," she replied.

More silence. Shifting, he finally asked, "What's wrong?"

She looked at him in pained reluctance. "I guess we need to talk."

11

Here it comes. Paul straightened slightly so that his stomach could make a clear drop of six inches. *The "we need to talk" conversation.*

The waitress chose this moment to put their plates in front of them, and Royce bent to pick up her purse from the floor. Paul watched over his steaming fajitas as she took out the battery receipt and her checkbook. Glancing at the receipt, she wrote out a check and extended it to him. He made no move to take it, eyeing her. "That was for Miriam's car."

"I know, but I owe her maintenance for carting me everywhere. Please take it, Paul." She pushed it toward him over the table. "I don't want to take advantage of you."

"How are you taking advantage of me?" he asked, jaw tight.

She inhaled. "I don't think . . . we should get back together."

He looked down at his plate momentarily. "Can you tell me why?"

"I just . . ." she faltered a little. "I just feel the need

to be on my own for a while. I've always been depend-ent on someone—Daddy, then Mack, then you—I really feel like I need to grow up and take care of myself for a change."

"Okay," he said woodenly, thinking, *You can't transport yourself or live by yourself, but you want to be independent?* It sounded like she was making excuses to him. "But, if you want a divorce, you're going to have to file. I'm not going to file," he added.

Her nod of assent crushed him.

The dinner was eaten in wretched silence, as there seemed to be nothing more to say. Paul paid the tab—another thirty bucks out of his dwindling cash—and they stood up to leave. Seeing her check still on the table, Royce picked it up, folded it, and tucked it into his shirt pocket, leaning forward to kiss him lightly on the lips. "Thank you for dinner." He glanced away.

Paul drove her back to her apartment; as there was no parking space close by, he parked in a visitor's spot and walked her to her door. She unlocked it, then turned to awkwardly squeeze his hand and murmur, "Thank you for everything, Paul. We'll keep in touch. I expect to hear how your new job works out!"

He nodded; she let herself into the apartment and closed the door.

Paul returned to the York. Since it suddenly seemed important to carry away something from his visits to the Old Book Shoppe, he studiously took the book upstairs. In the privacy of his closet, he plopped onto the bed and considered his course: he could dive headfirst into the beckoning pit of sorrow and self-pity, but what Harrison said—*"Have you learned anything or are you just bitter?"*—came back emphatically enough to make him pause. It meant something that he couldn't quite wrap his mind around. Was this supposed to be one of those learning experiences?

So, in studied defiance of his feelings, he put his second failed marriage out of his mind and stretched out on the bed to begin *The Aeneid*. He read how the gods, worshipped and feared, toyed with the lives of mortals— specifically, Aeneas—for their own ends, for jealousy, passion or rage:

From her old wound, the queen of gods compelled him—
    A man apart, devoted to his mission—
    To undergo so many perilous days
    And enter on so many trials. Can anger
    Black as this prey on the minds of heaven?

Paul read how Aeneas, battered and bleeding, set his face toward survival for the sake of not only himself and his crew, but for those he did not even know yet.

In the midst of his reading, Paul put the book down once, in order to set his phone alarm for five A.M. Whatever he did tomorrow, it seemed imperative that he get an early start doing it. He would *not* lie in bed all day. Most important, he was going to get use of the bathroom first.

In taking the phone out of his pocket, he found Royce's check. He paused to look it over—drawn on a Fort Worth bank, with her Eighth Avenue address— before tearing it up. Then he opened the book again and read until he fell asleep.

Five o'clock turned out to be plenty early to get the bathroom first the following morning, Wednesday. Paul leisurely showered and shaved, then scrupulously cleaned the tub and floor when he was through. He went downstairs to wait in the front parlor, reading the morning paper, until the breakfast buffet was open. He ate till he was stuffed, because they didn't serve lunch and he wasn't going to spend any more money on fast food. He only had about forty dollars left. (Then he realized that, with what Streiker had given him, his money had indeed held out until he had found her, ironically enough.)

By seven A.M., Paul was standing beside his truck, his great quest ended. Finding the desire of his heart—whatever that was—meant nothing now, because Royce didn't want him. He remembered vaguely that he was supposed to start at Worldwide Delivery Services today, but he didn't have it in him. He knew that delivering packages was not something he could do for very long. But if he didn't do that, he didn't know what else he should do, other than wait for Harrison to call him back. Waiting around for something to happen would not pay much, and he didn't want to continue to freeload at the York.

After a moment's reflection, he returned to his third-floor closet for the book. Tossing it on the floorboard, he made a deal with himself: if Worldwide Delivery called, he'd go in to work for them. If Harrison called, he'd do whatever he told him to. Whoever called first would get his services. "That great reward," he muttered ironically, turning the ignition.

But it was still just after seven. He merged into

downtown traffic, which was less gnarled than he expected, and drove to the warehouse district. Parking across the street from the Officina Gentium building, he surveyed the area. All looked deserted, as before, except the warehouse next door. It was fully lit and swarming with guys, even at this hour. But people who worked in the heat of a Texas summer learned to start early in the day.

Hesitantly, he got out of his truck, taking the book with him to approach the old warehouse headquarters of Officina Gentium. "I don't know where else to go," he conceded to himself. Part of his rationale in coming here was to be on the spot in case Harrison called. With misgiving, he reached out to the door, and opened it.

He looked into the dim, hot, stuffy interior. It was not yet light enough outside to much illumine the warehouse space through the grimy windows. And, since the air conditioning had been turned off, there were obviously no interviews planned for the next several hours. The place was uninhabitable even to sit and read, so Paul turned away.

On some kind of impulse, however, he turned back to step over the threshold, letting the door close behind him. *I have a right to be here.* It was not rational for him to think that one interview gave him free access, but—he did.

So he pressed the button to turn on the center row of lights as before. He paused to regard the surrounding rows of lights, surmising that they had been added at a later date, but not wired to the old button. He did not see how to turn them on. Nonetheless, the one row gave him enough light to begin looking for a thermostat.

He found it on the back wall, unlocked. So he turned on the air conditioning, listening to the hum of a powerful unit start up. The still air began circulating around him, and he let out his breath. Then his eye landed on the desk in the middle of the room, with the chair Harrison had sat in behind it—

In growing curiosity, Paul went over to examine this chair. It wasn't the one he had sat in to fill out the application. He could only assume it had been brought in for Harrison, as Paul hadn't paid any attention to it at the time. But it was a nice plush leather chair, with arms and a high back. The wooden chair that he had first sat in, which *might* have been the same one he sat in for the interview, was nowhere to be seen. The only chair here now was this nice cushy one.

Paul sat and rocked gently back. Given that it was altogether a fine reading chair, he threw his feet up on the desk, opened his book, and resumed reading where he had left off last night.

He read for two solid hours without stirring but to turn pages or shift his legs. While he was engrossed in Aeneas' story, he never noticed the air in the warehouse becoming comfortable, or the light from outside growing stronger.

But finally he had to lower the book and stretch. Dropping his feet to the concrete floor, he muttered, "Shouldn't've had all that coffee this morning. Now I have to go find a bathroom."

He stood, tossing the book on the desk. As he stepped away, a door on the back wall caught his eye. It didn't look like an exterior door, for some reason. Paul studied it, then went over and opened it. He stood looking into a small but clean bathroom with old-fashioned porcelain sink and commode. There was even a hip bath with a hand-held shower.

Stepping in and closing the door, Paul glanced around at the spare rolls of toilet paper, cleaning supplies, hand soap, and paper towels. He used the commode, which flushed properly, then he stood in front of the sink to wash his hands. He glanced at the drawn face and sad eyes that glanced back at him in the mirror, then dried his hands, depositing the used paper towels in the otherwise empty trash can.

He went back out to stand by the desk and just look around. All this empty space he found . . . comfortable. Being so far removed from the tiny living space he endured growing up, this was like . . . heaven, almost, in a stripped-down, urban kind of way.

Shaking his head, he began to settle back down at the desk when the front door opened. Paul looked up at a t-shirted man who stuck his head in. "You are here! I thought that was your truck outside. Saw you come in here yesterday. Hey, listen—I work at Bauhaus next door—we've got two guys that just dropped in the heat and a semi full of fresh seafood that has got to get unloaded into delivery trucks right away. Can you work? You'll get paid in cash."

"Sure," Paul said, stepping forward. Then he paused. "I'm waiting on a call about a job. If I get it, I'll have to leave."

"Well, just—come unload while you can." The guy waved him over urgently. "Cam Westford," he said, extending his hand as Paul approached.

"Paul Arrendondo." He briefly surveyed the other's

curly black hair, short beard, and crinkly eyes.

"Good to meet you, Paul." Exiting, Cam broke into a sprint toward the facility next door, and Paul followed, glimpsing the large, faded letters: Bauhaus Wholesale Seafood. They went around back to the huge loading bays, where a refrigerated eighteen-wheeler sat, its motor grumbling. A long line of smaller delivery trucks idled nearby, their drivers impatiently waiting.

Paul spotted a lift truck being driven away, and said, "Ah, I'm not qualified on a forklift."

"Don't need to be," Cam said. "Most of these are small orders going to area stores or restaurants for the day. All we need is good, old-fashioned back power. Seth!" he called, and a man in shirt and tie turned. "Got another pair of arms."

"Thank God for that. Always short-handed around here. Now, listen, Cam, you check his papers? He got a Social Security card? I don't want any trouble."

"Sure, Seth, sure," Cam said.

"Okay." Seth, habitually harried, gestured with a pen to a waiting truck. "Just fill their orders!"

Cam hopped up into the rear of the semi and pointed Paul to a white multistop truck painted with a grocer's logo. The driver, standing by the rear door, thrust a sheet at Paul as soon as he came within arm's length. Glancing down the form, he read, "Bauhaus: 1 shrimp, 1 flounder, 1 red snapper."

Running to the back of the semi, he handed the list up to Cam, who glanced at it and tossed it in a basket that held scores of similar forms, then removed one container from a stack and dropped it at the edge of the semi bed. It was insulated plastic, about two feet by two feet by eighteen inches, with a red lid and a label that said, "FRESH SHRIMP 10 doz." Also on the label was a stamp indicating the day and hour that the shrimp had been packed: "3:21 AM AUG 16"—today. The next container that Cam threw down had a green lid with the label, "FLOUNDER 2 doz." And the third container, identical in size and shape to the first two, was topped with a purple lid bearing the label: "RED SNAPPER 1 doz."

Because of their size, shape, and weight—about thirty-five pounds each—Paul could carry at most two at a time. The snapper and flounder went to the truck first, where the driver was waiting with open arms. Paul ran back for the shrimp; as soon as that was handed over and loaded, the driver slammed the door, hopped up in his cab, and departed. And Paul went to the next truck.

He soon learned several shortcuts: if Cam was engaged with another order, Paul could hop up in the bed and fetch the containers he needed, going only by the color of the lids; if Cam was free, Paul could shout out what he needed and basket the form himself. Two other Bauhaus employees were ostensibly doing the same thing, but with much less energy, as they didn't want to pass out in the heat. Due to Paul's efforts, the waiting trucks began to depart in a steady stream with their orders. One of those trucks, he noticed with interest, had the York B&B on their delivery route.

At one point, he paused, panting and dripping, to ask Cam, "Wouldn't it save a lot of time for the drivers to come get their own orders?"

"They're not allowed in the semi," Cam answered. Working in the back of the cool semi, he was in better shape. "We wouldn't know what all they took. And the containers can't sit on the ground. They have to stay totally clean."

Paul accepted that, continuing to run orders to the trucks despite his feet swelling in his boots. But he began to subconsciously search for a more efficient method of unloading.

An hour later he was soaked and trembling; Cam, sensing he was about to lose another body, gave him a bottle of water and put him in the back of the refrigerated semi. Here, Paul moved containers from their stacks closer to the door for others (who happened to not include Cam) to distribute to the customers' trucks.

Leaning over for the zillionth time, Paul suddenly saw his dripping shirt and his pocketed phone. "Yikes." He gingerly removed the phone, wiped it dry as best he could, then looked out of the semi at a departing back with free hands. "Hey!" Paul called, and the guy turned around.

Paul extended his phone. "Would you give that to Seth to hold for Paul?" The other took the phone and Paul watched long enough to see him head for Seth, standing with his clipboard in conference with the semi's driver. Then Paul went back to work, as new trucks with orders to be filled were arriving all the time.

Two hours later the last of the waiting trucks had received their orders. The remainder of the semi's load then had to be transferred to large refrigerators and/or freezers inside the warehouse for later customers. From random comments, Paul discovered these latecomers to be mostly representatives from processing plants that produced frozen seafood entrees.

At this point, Seth's secretary appeared with burgers and soft drinks for the crew. Paul, dragging himself to the shade of an overhang on the side of the warehouse, managed to claim the last burger. He sat on the ground in the shade to unwrap the burger and suck the paper cup dry, feeling his feet throb inside his boots. While he ate, Seth came over to regard him: "What's your name, again?"

"Paul Arrendondo." He let go of the burger with one hand to reach up and shake Seth's proffered hand.

"Well, Paul, I appreciate you coming over to give us a hand today," Seth said gravely. Fiftyish, solemn, continually in possession of a clipboard, he went on, "A lot of these seafood distributors, you know, they operate off the coast, and promise overnight delivery anywhere in the state. But they ship in regular trucks, you know, so even if the customer gets the order the next day, it's been sitting in a hot truck for who knows how long.

"We do it differently than everybody else, and our customers know it. Our seafood is packed in ice at the plant right on the water, then trucked up here where our customers can pick it up themselves. They count on us for the freshest seafood in the city. You saw that those trucks were from the best restaurants around. But it takes a lot of manpower to do it this way, and it's hard to find people willing to work."

"I see," Paul nodded, taking another large bite.

"Yes. So I'm just real pleased to find somebody who's not afraid to hustle," Seth said. For some reason, a clear picture of a muscular, resolute form appeared in Paul's mind, and he paused at the voiceless identification, *This is Aeneas.*

But Seth was continuing, "You'll be paid in cash as a contract employee, now. You'll be responsible for your own taxes. You understand?"

Paul gulped the rest of his burger and stood, wiping his hands on his jeans. "Yes, I do. I'm glad to help, and I'll work for you as long as I can, but I'm expecting—"

"Paul! You done?" Cam called.

"Yes. One second," Paul called back, then told Seth, "Please let me know if I get a call." Seth's heavy brows raised questioningly, but he nodded, so Paul went over to see what Cam needed him to do.

The job at hand was cleaning out one large freezer: hundreds of cartons of frozen seafood had to be transferred to two other freezers, the oldest cartons going in the front, and anything older than six months getting thrown out. So Paul spent the next three hours shivering in a wet shirt from one freezer to the next, hauling, rearranging, and discarding cartons.

While lifting one carton, he felt a painful twinge deep in his back which caused him to bobble the box momentarily. Setting it down, he put a hand on the pain. The slug from when Renetta accidentally shot him a year ago remained lodged inside him—the emergency-room doctor in Alpine had declined to remove it, as it was dangerously close to his aorta. But he had warned Paul that it should be taken out—if it shifted and pierced his aorta, he would die of internal hemorrhaging. Paul had never done anything about it, partly for the cost, partly in defiant fatalism: when his time came, that was as good a way as any to go. He gave himself thirty seconds for the pain to subside, then picked the box back up.

When he had completed that task, he presented his

slightly loopy self to Cam, who directed him to have a seat. Paul dropped into a folding chair to look vacantly around the warehouse. It was similar to the one next door, probably built around the same time, but how it compared in size he couldn't say, as this one was full and the other empty.

At one point he had to get up and move his chair to make room for a worker on an aluminum extension ladder. Craning his neck to look upward, Paul watched him resume attaching sections of PVC pipe together—it looked like he was installing a sprinkler system. *That's got to cost a bundle,* Paul mused. He found a safe place for his chair and sat back down in exhaustion.

Some minutes later Cam returned. Paul gestured upward: "That a sprinkler system going in?"

"Yeah." Cam turned an eye up to the installer high above them. "But it won't be done for another week and a half." Why this should displease Cam, Paul didn't ask, for he noticed that Cam was carrying cash. Paul watched in tired interest as Cam plopped 5 twenties in his hand. "You hustled good for us, Paul. Any time you need work, come back here."

"Right," Paul groaned, standing, and shoved the cash in his back pocket. "I'll just go cancel my gym membership now." Cam laughed, patting his shoulder, whereupon Paul dragged himself out to his truck. Bleary-eyed, he focused on his watch: 4:45. Then he turned the ignition and drove semi-alertly back to the York.

Finding the third-floor bath empty, he grabbed fresh clothes from a suitcase and commandeered the bathroom to clean up. He pulled off his boots, groaning at the new blisters: footwear that was good on a ranch was not meant for concrete.

He finished stripping to bathe. However, he forgot to lock the door, so while he was showering, someone came in and used the commode. Despite the blast of cold water that hit him when the intruder flushed, Paul didn't care. He was too tired.

Aching in every cell of his body, but presentable to civilization, he stopped by his room to drop dirty clothes on the floor. Then he paused over the note left on his bed: "Mr. Arrendondo. Please see Mrs. Nicholas."

With a twinge of concern, he hastened downstairs and looked into the office off the parlor. "Mrs. Nicholas? You wanted to see me?"

"Yes, I do, Mr. Arrendondo." She looked up with a vaguely troubled smile. "I'm afraid we have a horde of guests arriving tomorrow. Unbelievable as it may seem, we're going to need your cubbyhole."

"I'll be out tonight," Paul said, backing up.

"No, no, stay the night. If you can be out by checkout tomorrow—eleven—that will be adequate."

"Thank you. I'll be out hours before then. Thank you for accommodating me." He reached out to shake her hand over her desk.

"You're welcome. I believe the dinner buffet is open," she nodded.

"I'll go see if that's a fact," he said, and found it to be true.

He was surprised to find that he wasn't all that hungry, so settled on salad, bread, and fresh shrimp cocktail (which was excellent).

Then he dragged himself up the stairs, contemplating, *Well, the free ride's over. Didn't last long. It's kind of a relief—I don't like sponging off people. At least I earned some living money today. But I didn't hear from*—At that, he slapped his empty shirt pocket in recollection: Seth had his phone. "Aw, [expletive]," he muttered. Bauhaus would be closed by now. He'd have to go get the phone tomorrow.

By the time he got to his room and sat on the bed, he realized that he'd left *The Aeneid* behind, as well. This almost dismayed him more than not having his phone for the night. He really wanted to read more—something of himself was now vested in Aeneas. Oh, well. He'd just have to get both tomorrow. So he flopped back on the bed and passed out.

In the morning he startled up, groping for the light button on his watch: 5:45. He turned on the room light and groggily gathered his clothes in his suitcases. He made sure the room was relatively neat—all trash in the can and not on the floor beside it—and carried his suitcases downstairs. No one was at the check-in desk, and Mrs. Nicholas' office door behind it was closed. So Paul left his key on the desk and departed the York.

He bought his standard fast-food biscuits and coffee, which he ate in the truck, then drove to the warehouse district. As he surmised, Bauhaus was already lit and operational. Paul parked across the street and entered, looking for Seth.

Cam met him first: "Paul! Great! Now we'll get done two hours early!"

Paul laughed, "Well, I'm not really here to work today. Where's Seth? He has my phone."

"Seth has your phone?" Cam said, and Paul nodded.

"Huh. Let me go ask him," Cam said.

So Paul watched the unloading (which was proceeding at less than peak efficiency) while Cam went to the office in the front of the warehouse. In a few minutes he returned with Seth. Paul watched his empty-handed approach in mild concern. "Hello, Paul. Good to see you today. What's this about your phone?"

"I—gave one of the guys my phone to give to you while I was working yesterday," Paul said, a sinking feeling in his stomach.

Seth shook his head. "No one gave me a phone to hold. Who'd you give it to?"

"Oh, man." Paul sagged. "It was—I thought it was one of the crew. I don't know his name."

Cam eyed him sympathetically. "That wasn't real bright, Paul. People sometimes slip back here during unloading to see what they can make off with. When we're busy, we can't always go around checking IDs."

Paul shook his head. "That's my fault. I just gave away my phone."

Cam offered, "Another day's work will earn you enough to replace it."

"Yeah, I guess I'd better. Just—let me leave a note next door, in case Mr. Harrison comes by when he can't reach me on my phone. I'll be right back."

"Good," Seth nodded, turning away.

So Paul sprinted to his truck, berating himself on the way. He yanked off his boots to don athletic shoes from his suitcase, then retrieved his pen and one of his research sheets before locking the truck back up with his bags inside. He tentatively opened the door to the Officina Gentium warehouse—was it always unlocked?

—and hurried back to the desk. Intent on looking for his book, he failed to notice that he had left the lights and air conditioning on yesterday. To his relief, the book was still on the desk where he had left it.

On the back of his list of Streiker companies in Fort Worth, Paul wrote, "Aug. 17. Mr. Harrison: I lost my phone working at Bauhaus yesterday—am working there again today, so please contact me there if you need me. Thank you, Paul." Something else occurred to him, and he impulsively added, "P.S. I also had to vacate my room at the York, so if you know of anyplace cheap I could stay, I'd appreciate it."

This he left out on the desk, along with the pen, then headed for the door. He was not particularly looking forward to another day of hard physical labor, but it was better than sitting around waiting and brooding, especially without a phone. (How could he have been so stupid?) So he presented himself to Cam, who immediately sent him to the next multistop truck waiting for their order of fresh seafood.

Two hours later, while Paul was running containers of crab, flounder, red and black drum, oysters, red snapper, sea trout, and especially shrimp to customers' trucks, Royce and Miriam were getting ready for another work day. As Miriam was putting on makeup, she was discoursing about one of the doctors at the hospital where her mother was being treated. "He's single, with one child, a little girl. He brought her up to the hospital yesterday, so I was able to get in good with her. I saw her run back and tell him how nice I was."

"Is this 'Doctor Bear'?" Royce asked, sitting to pull on pantyhose.

"Yes," Miriam giggled. "It's his nickname up at the hospital. I thought it was because he's so sweet and cuddly, but then he told me it had to do with his name, and I'm like, 'duh, how dumb of me,' but he thought I was cute."

"Of course you're cute. Listen, how's your mom?"

"Actually, she's a lot better. It's amazing. My brother Carter says she'll probably go home tomorrow. They want to keep her overnight for observation. Oh, he looked at the battery Paul got, and said it was fine, but he was really upset that Paul didn't take the car in for a tune-up while he was at it."

"Oh?" Royce said, mildly disturbed.

Miriam glanced at her. "The car really needs a tune-up."

Royce looked up. "Oh. I need to take care of that, don't I?"

"I'd appreciate it," Miriam said frankly.

"Okay. No problem," Royce said, a little worriedly.

"When?"

"I'm sorry?" Royce looked up again.

"When can you take the car in for a tune-up?" Miriam said, a little exasperated.

For a nondriver who wasn't even clear on how to gas up a car, the prospect of taking one in for a "tune-up" was daunting. And, as usual, Royce's checkbook was at a low ebb. She rather hoped Paul would wait a few days to cash her check. "Oh. Well." Her brow furrowed. "Since I took sick days, I'm not off again until Monday."

"Royce," Miriam exhaled, turning in her chair, "can't you ask Paul to do it?"

"Oh, dear. I don't want to do that," Royce breathed. "How would that make him feel?—I just told him we're not getting back together."

"So? Isn't he concerned enough about you as a friend to help with this kind of thing? Besides, you paid him for the battery; you can pay him for this, too," Miriam argued.

"I can offer, but I'm not sure he'd take it," Royce said hesitantly.

"Well, I wish you'd just ask him. That may be the only way this maintenance gets done," Miriam pointed out.

"Oh, I'm sorry. I know I promised to take care of it," Royce fretted.

She resumed dressing, and Miriam said nothing else while she sat at her computer to check the morning news headlines and her e-mail.

But when they got into the car, and Miriam started up the engine to a painfully rough idle, Royce took out her phone, scrolled through the numbers, and dialed. Miriam, looking satisfied, pulled out of the parking lot toward work.

On the way, she turned on the radio, permanently set to the classical music station out of Dallas. One reason she and Royce got along so famously was because they both loved classical music—and hated country western.

A minute later Royce closed the phone and replaced it in her purse. Miriam glanced at her and turned the radio down. "Well?"

"He's not picking up," Royce said, turning hurt eyes toward the side window.

"You didn't leave a message," Miriam observed.

"He knows my number. He knows that would be me calling," Royce said.

"Maybe he can't answer right now. Leave a message," Miriam instructed, at the end of her patience.

So Royce got the phone back out and redialed. Clearing her throat, she said, "Um, hi, Paul. I . . . have a favor to ask. I'd appreciate a call back. Thanks." Then she closed the phone, troubled.

12

While the sun rose to cook everything exposed to it, Paul ran containers of seafood to the waiting drivers. Only today, no one was in the back of the semi; Paul had to retrieve the containers himself and get them to the trucks. He looked up once or twice to see Cam lolling in the shade with another employee, letting Paul do most of the work. It irked him a little, but with the restaurant trucks waiting, and Seth looking anxiously out from time to time, Paul just did what needed to be done until the last of the trucks had rambled off.

Cam offered him a bottle of water off a rack and let him rest in the shade for a minute, then produced a list to direct which remaining containers went to freezers 3 and 4, and which went to refrigerator 2. This was not a matter of tossing cartons into a walk-in and walking away; anything left in the refrigerator from the previous day had to be thrown out, and anything placed in a freezer required that all existing stock in that freezer be rotated toward the front. Since the freezers could be left open for only minutes at a time, it had to be done quickly.

The task was made easier by the fact that containers sharing a packing date went on the same rolling shelf, so shelves were merely rolled in and rolled forward. At the same time, the task was made harder because of the sloppy manner it had been done in the past. But due to Paul's work the previous day, no containers in freezer 3 had to be tossed, which saved him work today.

Seth bought the crew pizza for lunch—and suddenly a whole pack of men whom Paul had not seen working at all that morning showed up. Waiting for his turn at the lunch table, Paul leaned against the wall; at the jab in his shoulder he moved, looking back at the fire alarm he'd leaned against. He glanced around the warehouse space, counting four pull alarms within his sight. He looked up to the ceiling, noting the progress on the sprinkler system. It was easy to see why Cam was anxious: they had a huge expanse of ceiling yet to cover to get it all done within ten days. Then Paul wondered if such precautions were standard.

When he finally got to the lunch table, he loaded a paper plate with pepperoni slices and went back to the wall to sit on the concrete floor with his plate and a soft drink. Cam amiably sat beside him with a similar plate, and Paul mumbled, "Sure is nice of Seth to spring for lunch. He do this every day?"

"Uh huh," Cam answered, mouthing hot cheese. "Found out that it saved money to feed everybody and get them right back to work."

"Yeah." Paul withheld comment on how much everybody worked. "Hey, the sprinkler system must cost a bundle. Is that to bring the building up to code, or what?"

Cam looked up, wiping cheese from his beard. "The answer to that would be, 'what.' We've got this ongoing thing with punks breaking in, looting the office, and setting fires. Seth started taking the petty cash box home with him every day and hired night security, or tried to. It's tough getting someone willing to work."

"I guess so," Paul said. Touching his empty pocket where his phone used to reside, he worried a little bit about Mr. Harrison trying to call. While Paul was grateful for this work—and to be able to work—if he wanted to haul around boxes for a living, he would've gone to work for Worldwide Delivery. As it was, they couldn't call him either, so he was really counting on Harrison to come by the warehouse.

Paul also began to worry a little about where he would sleep tonight; he didn't know if the Get Happy people were still happily monopolizing all hotel space, but—any place he had to pay for, he couldn't afford, so he put off thinking about that.

They finished their pizza, then Cam set him to sweeping the rear of the warehouse—hundreds of square feet of concrete. Paul used a push broom to sweep dirt and debris into a tilt truck, which he then rolled out back and up a ramp. From there, it could be emptied directly into the city-owned dumpster. As much as he swept, however, it still smelled bad back here. *This is what I'm doing with a master's in divinity*, Paul thought idly. *Wouldn't Papa be proud.*

On his second or third trip up the ramp, he paused to scan the rear of the Officina Gentium warehouse to his right. A chain-link fence topped with barbed wire separated and enclosed both rear lots, comprising the bays and wide driveways. The barbed wire was probably necessary, Paul reflected. He believed Cam, that there was always somebody cruising deserted areas looking for anything of takeaway value—and he kicked himself again for losing his phone.

When he had finished that chore, he replaced the equipment in a storage closet and went to find Cam. Seeing him talking to another of the crew, Paul leaned against the wall to wait—after making sure that a fire alarm wasn't behind him.

Eventually, Cam glanced over at him and said, "I guess we've worked you enough for one day, huh? Sit tight there a second." Paul took him literally, sliding down the wall to sit on the floor. His back hurt, his gut hurt, his feet hurt—and he was suddenly glad to be pushing a broom so that he didn't have to think about how much his heart hurt. Walt had put him to work when Kris left him; now Bauhaus gave him the opportunity to get over Royce's leaving.

Coming over with Paul's pay for the day, Cam chortled and offered him a hand up from the floor. Paul stood, grunting, and pocketed the cash. "Hey, listen, a couple of us are going out for a beer. Hang around for a minute and go with us," Cam invited.

Paul looked at him in grateful surprise. "Thanks for the offer. Another time. I've got to—" he broke off, unwilling to tell Cam that he had to find someplace to sleep tonight. "I've got some stuff to take care of tonight. But thanks."

Cam nodded, and Paul lumbered out. His muscles felt like spaghetti. He was tired of constantly smelling his own sweat. He was anxious about missing a call from Harrison. But he had earned another hundred dollars. He thought he knew hard work at the ranch—and it was true that he sometimes put in 16-hour days. But much of that time was eaten up leisurely riding from one part of the pasture to another, shooting the breeze with Walt. Paul suddenly missed that life very much.

After reassuring himself that his truck had not been tampered with, he returned to the Officina warehouse. Upon opening the door, he sighed in gratitude at the comfortable coolness of the building. Then he felt guilty about leaving the air conditioning running—it must cost a bundle to air condition all this empty space. *Then* he noticed that there was additional furniture along the back wall of the warehouse.

Goaded by curiosity, Paul covered the expanse of floor at a trot. There, against the back wall, was an iron-frame bed with mattress, sheets, and pillow. It was not a big bed—merely a twin—but it was clearly an invitation to make himself at home. Paul sat on the mattress, finding it reasonably comfortable, and noted the reading lamp affixed to the head of the bed. His copy of *The Aeneid* lay on the pillow. Paul picked up the book, tapping it on his leg, then leaned over to see the cord of the reading lamp plugged into a wall socket. Everything had been made ready for him.

He looked back to the desk, still in the middle of the floor 75 feet away. It made no sense to have everything so spread out. So, leaving the book on the bed, he went back to the desk and took hold of one side preparatory to dragging it. That was when he noticed that the note he had left this morning was gone, replaced by two other items.

First, there was a key, which Paul picked up. It was a large, old-fashioned key on a chain with a heavy bronze tag. Stamped on one side of the tag were the ornate letters *OG*—for Officina Gentium, no doubt. Paul weighed this in his hand a moment—was this a hint to start locking the door?—then put it down to pick up the second item: a remote control with a row of buttons, unmarked.

The first button was larger than the others, with four directional arrows pointing outward from the center. Paul tentatively pushed the up arrow, and two rows of lights over his head came on, in addition to the center row. Pushing the other directional arrows in turn caused succeeding rows of lights to come on. Pushing them again toggled the rows off.

Paul played with the lights for a while, discovering the combinations to make a particular row go on or off, or all of them go on or off. He finally left all off but the center row, the most practical for his needs. He glanced up at the old light button by the door, still connected to these basic lights.

When he pushed the second button on the remote, he heard the air conditioning condenser stop humming. He quickly toggled that back on again. The next row comprised three buttons, the first being larger than the other two. He pressed the big button, and was badly startled by a loud rattle behind him. Wheeling, he watched a large bay door in the back wall roll up on its track, exposing the driveway and rear bay.

Paul walked out through this door to scrutinize the drive. It sloped down, then to the right around the corner of the building. To his left were two loading docks, raised off the ground to provide level unloading from 18-wheelers. He pressed one of the smaller buttons to confirm that they opened and closed these two bay doors. Then he followed the sloping drive around to a closed gate. Seeing wheels on the bottom of the gate, he pressed the last button on the remote, and the gate rolled open to the side.

He evaluated all this, then went out to his truck across the street. He climbed in, started it up, and drove it through the gate and up the ramp into the warehouse. He closed the gate and the bay door via the remote, then hauled his suitcases out of the truck to place them beside the bed. On a thought, he took the heavy old key to the front door to confirm that this key locked and unlocked it. Then he sat on his bed and looked at his truck. He hardly knew what to make of all this.

So he got up to flip open a suitcase for some fresh clothes, and took them with him into the small bathroom, quietly thrilled at the privacy. The hand shower in the hip bath worked just fine; since he had forgotten to pack shampoo, he reached over for the dispenser of hand soap on the sink, and that worked fine, too.

He dried off and dressed, cleaning up after himself as if he were still at the York, then emerged from the bath in a persistent stupor. Surveying the warehouse, he embarked on a comprehensive tour.

He had already located the wall thermostat; next to it was the multi-switchplate for the lights. There was a large utility closet with cleaning equipment, ladders, hand tools, and such. He also discovered the water-heater closet and a separate room that housed the massive air-conditioning and heating units, as well as an electric generator. The warehouse generated its own power. He investigated several other closets, each about ten by twenty feet, and that was it.

His stomach started growling, so, armed with the remote, he climbed in his truck, U-turned comfortably, and drove on down the ramp and out the gate to the first sandwich shop he could find. Then he brought his dinner back to his new quarters. Passing Bauhaus, he noted that it was closed. He slowed his truck to see the security guard sitting in his car at the curb, reading. Paul tiredly shook his head: the guard should be out walking around the building.

Paul opened the gate with the remote, pulled on up the ramp, and got out of his truck to stand beside his bed. He laughed, "A cowboy loves his truck, but this is weird." He went to the desk in the middle of the space to drag it closer to his little grouping as he had first intended to, then sat at the desk to eat his dinner in a contemplative haze.

Wadding up the trash, he looked around, and got up to fetch a circular metal trash can from one of the utility closets. On second thought, he rummaged through the shelves until he had located trash-can liners. Thus he was able to deposit his trash in a lined can. Then he looked around, muttering, "Would be nice to have a beer about now. A cold one." And he regarded the wall socket into which the reading light had been plugged.

Fed and comfortable, he looked at his poor old truck again. Setting his jaw, he went to one of the storage closets to bring out rubber gloves, a bristle brush, and an array of cleaners. Then he donned the gloves, threw open both cab doors and went to work on the bench seat.

Fortunately, the excrement had not drained into the crack between the seat and the back, so Paul was able to reach all of the residue without dismantling anything. He scrubbed it fiercely, trying first one cleanser, then another. By the time he had rinsed everything away, the stain was gone, replaced by a large bleached spot. And, it no longer smelled bad. It smelled powerfully disinfected, which was far preferable to how it smelled before.

Satisfied, he put everything away, took off his shoes, and scrunched up the pillow against the head of the bed. Flopping against it, he turned off the warehouse lights and clicked on the reading lamp.

The moment he was in bed, alone, his losses blindsided him, as they tended to do whenever he let down his guard. It was bad enough that Walt died, but at least he hadn't intended to betray Paul this way. But Royce—the pain, the anger, the bitterness of losing her sat all together on his chest to stab him repeatedly: *She doesn't want you. She doesn't need you. Just go die.*

As something of a shield, everything Harrison had said came back to him; that, combined with the bed beneath him—evidence that someone thought him worth keeping around—helped deflect the attack.

Deliberately, he opened *The Aeneid* to resume reading where he had left off. The words were a solace; sliding into Aeneas' skin enabled him to shed the discomfort of his own. Tired as he was, however, after ten pages the words started to blur on the page, and he put his head down, reaching up to turn off the light.

The moment Royce got off work that evening, she checked her phone for messages. There was nothing from Paul. She stewed about it until Miriam picked her up. While Royce was settling in the passenger seat, Miriam asked, "So, is Paul going to take the car in for you?"

"I don't know," Royce said tightly. "He hasn't called me back." She pretended that it didn't bother her, and Miriam said nothing on the short ride to their apartment. As soon as they got home, however, Royce shut herself out on the tiny back patio and dialed. She listened to Paul's script, the same as before: "This is Paul. Leave a message."

She took the phone away from her ear to press 1, prompting the beep, and said, "Paul, it's Royce. Look, I'm—sorry if I hurt you. Even if we don't stay married, I didn't intend for you to just go away. I don't see why we can't talk. I would really appreciate a call back." Then she terminated the call with a twinge of righteous indignation that he wasn't jumping when she pulled his leash.

Re-entering the apartment, she told Miriam, "Okay, he should call back once he gets off work. I'm sure he hasn't called because he's been at work."

"Okay, good. I'm going up to the hospital," Miriam said, applying lipstick with the aid of a lighted mirror.

Royce paused, looking confused. "I thought your mom went home today."

"No, no, tomorrow," Miriam purred, checking the back of her dress. "I've got one more day to work on him! Wish me luck!" She crossed her fingers. "And don't wait up."

After Miriam had left, Royce, without wheels, scrounged up something for dinner from what they had in the cabinets. Keeping her phone within hearing range, she picked up a very interesting novel that she had found at the book shop and read industriously for about ten minutes, but the characters were all doing something that she had no interest in at all, so she turned on the TV, but she and Miriam couldn't afford cable on top of everything else, so there was nothing much interesting on, so she drew herself a nice bubble bath in which to luxuriate, but the bathroom was small and not very clean, so that was not as enjoyable an experience as she would have liked.

But since she had gone to the trouble to draw the water and all, she was determined to *make* herself enjoy it. So she leaned back on the bath pillow and closed her eyes to listen to the Bach that drifted in from the bedroom radio. All was well until the music ended and a commercial came on—a loud, grating commercial of LOUD, GRATING country music—on the classical station! Royce almost slid off the air pillow in aggravation.

Glaring toward the bedroom, she suddenly remembered that Paul liked country music, somewhat. But whenever she came into a room to hear country playing on the Ferrings' satellite system, he'd reach over and change the station, or turn it off. He even did that when Walt was in the room listening to it. But Walt didn't care—at least, he never complained, not as much as Royce. No one complained as much as she did.

Involuntarily, she remembered how bone-tired Paul was those last few weeks before she'd left—she could still see him fighting to stay awake while she vented her displeasure over petty grievances he had no power to correct. What had she done to help him?

Once or twice he had started to talk about how Walt was flagging, but she hadn't really listened. She hadn't cared that much . . . and now Walt was dead. She thought about Jeannine's saying how good Paul was for Walt, how he gave Walt some much-needed male companionship, even a sense of purpose. Little did Royce realize that Walt had done the same for Paul.

She looked down at the glistening soap bubbles, understanding for the first time what a blow Walt's death must have been to her husband. And she wasn't there to help him through it. Even now, all that mattered was what he could do for her. . . .

Royce decided she was through with the bath. So she got out of the tub and put on silk pajamas (that Paul had bought for her). She stripped off her old fingernail polish and applied a new coat, then watched about thirty minutes of snowy television waiting for her nails to dry. Finally she tucked herself into bed.

Ten minutes later she sat up, turned on the light, and picked up her phone. She dialed a number, listened to the message in burgeoning exasperation, then said, "Paul, this is not about the car—I don't care if you take it in for a tune-up or not. It's just not right for you to go to all that trouble to find me and then vanish again just because I didn't jump into bed with you. Will you please just call me back?"

She replaced the phone on the bedside table, positioning it right next to her head, then turned off the light and flounced back down. How could she apologize for anything if he wouldn't call her back? And the countering question crossed her mind, *It's still all about you, isn't it?*

She only pretended to be asleep when Miriam tiptoed in hours later.

The next morning Paul was awakened by thumping that resonated through the empty, echoing warehouse. "Uh?" He opened his eyes in the darkness, rolling off the bed to fumble for the remote. A barrage of lights came on at his command, then he found his watch to bring it within view. "Oh, for pity's sake," he groaned.

He stumbled across the expanse of concrete at the continued pounding and opened the front door. "Cam, what the—? It's five A.M.!"

"Yeah, and if you come now, there's a bonus," Cam replied. "Listen, it'd be nice not to have to come get you every day like this."

"Cam." Paul leaned wearily against the doorframe. "You woke me up. I haven't had any breakfast."

"Seth has pancakes, eggs, bacon, juice and coffee, but it goes to the first guys who come in."

Paul's eyes came into immediate focus. "I'll be right there." He closed the door and ran back for shoes—not his boots, obviously, which he had learned not to wear after the first day—but his athletic shoes. Since he'd slept in his clothes (again) he was already dressed. He stuffed the OG key into his back pocket, then paused over the desk.

He retrieved another sheet from the floorboard of the clean-smelling truck—the original list of clinics that Mitch had given him. Paul flipped it over and wrote: "Mr. Harrison: thank you for the accommodations. I sure would appreciate a visit to discuss my future with this company. I've been working next door at Bauhaus, so am available after 4 p.m. Thanks again, Paul."

He struggled for a few seconds over what might be presumptuous, then added, "P.S. The bed is great. Is there any way to get a refrigerator in here? Also—my phone was stolen. I really need one, but my credit cards are maxed out. ~~Anything you can do~~" He decided that he'd begged enough, and left it at that.

Then Paul hurried next door, where the multistop trucks were already lining up in the brightly lit bays to await the arrival of the semi with its fresh seafood. He wolfed down breakfast, eyeing the trucks. Everybody was just standing around, including the Bauhaus crew. Everybody thought they had to wait on the semi to do anything.

Paul took a huge gulp of black coffee, tossed the cup, and wiped his hands on his jeans. Then he went to the small office, looking for Seth or Cam. Not seeing either, he appropriated a sheaf of blank white paper and a couple of thick black markers. These he took around to the waiting trucks.

At the first truck, he took the driver's order sheet, marking it with a big black "1," circled. On a blank paper he wrote a seven-inch-high "1." This number he gave to the driver, telling him, "Hold it up when we start unloading. I'll call you over to get your own order."

"Good!" the driver said.

Paul went to the next truck, marking his order with a "2," giving him a corresponding number, and telling him the same thing. He went on down the line doing this until he had collected the first ten orders.

At that time the semi rolled up. While the driver pulled it into position, Paul grouped his orders according to likeness—the customers who wanted nothing but shrimp went in one group; the customers who wanted crab and flounder went together, and so on. Then he fetched ten or twelve pallets, setting them on the ground behind the 18-wheeler. By the time the back doors of the semi swung open, Paul was ready.

He hopped up to begin grouping containers in the respective orders right there in the back of the truck— the big issue with fresh seafood being that, even packed in ice and insulated, it could not be left out for any length of time, according to Seth's scruples.

So when Paul had the first order collected, he hauled the containers out and set them on pallets on the ground next to the semi. He checked it over to make sure it was complete, wrote a big "1" on the side of the top container, then whistled for the driver, who was anxiously holding up his number like a bidder at auction. The driver and his helper ran forward to collect their containers.

Several paces apart, Paul unloaded customer number 2's order, then waved for him. By the time Paul got the third and fourth orders out, the Bauhaus crew (not being overly industrious by nature) began to drift over from breakfast. Seeing Paul bring the containers off the semi in orderly groups, they naturally fell to assisting the drivers load up their purchases. The trucks began peeling off the line with clocklike regularity.

Paul conscripted one of Bauhaus' crew who was a little more alert than the rest, a guy by the name of Sean, to assign numbers and bring him the orders. Then he required only one other set of hands to transfer the grouped, numbered containers to pallets, ready for pick-up by the waiting drivers.

As all this was falling into place, Paul was too busy to see that Cam had come out to watch. Minutes later, he departed, reappearing with Seth, who stood and watched. Then Seth turned to Cam and started talking voluminously and vehemently for such a mild-mannered guy. He found reason to gesture toward Paul several times. Cam hung his head, listening.

The unloading was completed hours earlier than usual. Some of the crew that had sat around in the shade the whole time were sent home by Seth, permanently.

Following lunch, Cam set Paul to work cleaning out refrigerator 1. Instead of just moving stuff around (as some guys tended to do) Paul went through the containers one by one. Because many of them had been opened and some of the packages removed, the only way to tell *for sure* which were still good was to put human eyes on them. Paul took a clipboard into the refrigerator with him, to inventory while he was cleaning.

Midafternoon, Paul handed his inventory to Cam, who took it to Seth in his office. A few minutes later, Cam returned with his cash for the day: $300. Paul sifted through the twenties, eyeing him. "This is a lot more than you've been paying me."

"Tomorrow's Saturday—our busiest day of the week. Seth wants to know if you can be here at five," Cam said.

Paul hesitated. He was tired of this work and didn't want to do it anymore. But what else was there for him to do? "Yeah, if nobody from my other job contacts me."

He did not really believe anybody would, at this point. The communication seemed to be all rather one-sided.

"Good. We're closed on Sunday. Listen, the guys are meeting at Baby's Cantina tonight, if you want to come," Cam added.

"Before a five-A.M.-workday?" Paul asked wryly.

"We pack it in early," Cam reassured him.

"Thanks. If I can stay awake, I'll come," Paul said.

"Good," Cam said, so Paul betook himself wearily next door.

He grabbed the doorknob and yanked as usual, almost bashing his face into the unmoving door with the force of his pull. It was locked! He gaped at it a moment, then brought out the key from his back pocket to unlock the door and open it.

Mulling over the sudden security of a locked door, he glanced up and startled. Was that a—? Forgetting his fatigue, he trotted forward to examine the new appliance standing against the wall near the bed. "They did! They put a refrigerator in here!" he exclaimed, running a hand over the small, white, old-fashioned box refrigerator. It looked very much like the one his parents owned, except it was clean.

Paul opened it. And it cooled. It was already functional, though empty. He eagerly looked on the desk to see what else they might have left, but there was nothing. Just to be sure, he opened all the drawers—still nothing. He was a little disappointed, hoping to have found a phone as well, but . . . the refrigerator he intended to put to good use.

Invigorated, he showered and changed, then got in his nice clean truck to go buy a pizza and two six-packs of beer. As he returned with his food, plopping the pizza box on the desk and stashing the beers in the fridge, he wondered, *Who's doing this? And . . . why?*

That morning, when Royce found no message on her phone from Paul, she quietly put it away and did not check it the rest of the day. But while she worked, restocking shelves and helping customers find books, she thought about him. She thought about how good he looked all geared up to go work in the pasture. Once when he caught her eyeing him strapping on chaps, he grinned in his devilish way and murmured, *"I'm comin' to bed tonight wearin' nothin' but these"*—as he slapped the chaps.

Royce laughed out loud at the remembrance, then glanced around to see if anyone in the next aisle heard. Seeing no one, she returned to her reverie. Of course, that night he had come in and fallen asleep in the shower. While waiting for him to come to bed, she'd grown concerned over the length of time she heard the shower running. When she went to check on him, she found him literally asleep on his feet. So she had turned off the water, dried him off, and tucked him in bed. He rolled over to hold her, but that was all. He always loved to hold her at night.

And whenever he came in from the pasture, he always checked first to see where she was and if she needed anything. Grasping a book to her chest, she remembered his appearing in the house with bleeding cuts from barbed wire only to be accosted by her demands. So what did he do? Right where he stood, he pulled out his phone and called a friend of Jeannine's to see where she had bought some shoes that Royce lusted after.

How could she have turned her back on someone like that? So she thought about the day she finally left—what was it that had pushed her over the edge?

Standing in the empty reading niche, Royce stared down at the book she had picked up to reshelf—it was titled *My Mother, Myself*. With palpitating heart, she remembered: it wasn't anything Paul had done; it was something Jeannine had said—something about the short skirt Royce had worn into town. *"People in a small town can be—judgmental about little things like that, Royce."*

Obviously, it had been intended as a friendly heads-up regarding unfriendly gossip, but in Royce's hyper-sensitive state of mind, it sounded like the cutting comments that her mother used to make. So Royce had interpreted it as such, decided she was too sophisticated for small-town life, and . . . left. Without a word to him, without a word to anyone.

Royce raised watering eyes to the books on the orderly shelf, each where it should be. How unfair was it of her to do that to him? Then when he called, trying to find out what was wrong, she wouldn't pick up. (The next day her phone had been stolen.)

Was that ironic now, or what?—that he was doing the same thing: not picking up her calls. The difference was, he was justified. He had spent a lot of time and effort tracking her down, only for her to tell him she was perfectly fine without him, thank you. What should she have expected? That he would hang around, waiting on her hand and foot in hopes that she might change her mind?—because honestly, that *is* what she had been expecting. She knew Paul; she knew how desperately he needed to be loved, so she was counting on his need to keep him hanging around until she decided what suited her.

"Selfish, selfish bit—" she murmured in remorse, closing her eyes. For whatever reason, he had found the strength not to play that game. And now she was very sorry that she had initiated it.

When she clocked out that day, she finally checked her phone. Her heart leaped when she saw, "1 missed call." She pressed the message button, held the phone to her ear with trembling fingers, and heard: "—sorry we missed you. Our truck will be in your area tomorrow, Saturday, August nineteenth, so if you have any gently used clothing or household items to contribute, please call our toll-free line—" Royce quietly pushed the "end" button and put away her phone.

When Miriam picked her up a few minutes later, she was gushing good news: "My doctor called me at lunch today! He's meeting me at Don Pablo's tonight! Oh, I think this is it! What do you think I should wear—the slinky red or the little black dress?"

Royce blinked rapidly. Having lost the opportunity to be a friend to the one person in her life who deserved it most, she determined to be a friend to anyone else she could find. "Honestly? You look drop-dead gorgeous in the little black number, but it's too dressy for Don Pablo's. I'd go with the red."

"You're probably right," Miriam said, accelerating to beat a yellow light. The engine pinged loudly, but she never noticed. Cutting a sideways glance at her passenger, she added, "Problem is, I don't have any accessories that look right with it."

Royce tsked in disapproval. "Well, we can't send you out on such an important mission unequipped, can we? Wear my drop earrings."

Miriam squealed, "I was hoping you'd offer, so I wouldn't have to beg. You know how proud I am."

"Yeah," Royce smiled. "Listen, did your mom get home all right today?"

Miriam reached over to squeeze her hand. "Yes, Carter took her home, and she's resting comfortably. You're such a dear to ask."

"Um hmm," Royce murmured, listening to the engine knocking. They stopped to get a to-go salad for Royce (while the car "dieseled"—continued to run for a second after being shut off) then hurried back to the apartment for Miriam to get ready. Royce played maid, styling Miriam's hair, finding the drop earrings, and making sure the dress was spotless and lint-free.

An hour later Miriam sailed out, blowing a kiss. "Don't wait up!"

"Just take notes, to tell me all about it tomorrow," Royce said, waving. And she closed the door with a great sense of heaviness. Paul would be taking her out tonight, if she had only let him. So was her life any better now than it had been on the ranch?

She sat heavily at the tea table, taking her phone out of her purse. Not surprised to see 0 messages, she sighed, playing with the keypad. She idly dialed in Paul's number and listened.

Then she closed it again without leaving a message. "If only . . . oh, I wish I could tell him what I've learned.

If I could just catch him in person, maybe he'd talk to me. Even when he was out on the pasture with his hands full of barbed wire, he would always stop what he was doing to talk to me. He was always so good about listening. . . ."

She began mulling over everything they had talked about when he brought her dinner Monday. Gradually, her vision focused, and she began thinking out loud. "He said he had applied for a job in town. He said he was staying someplace in town . . . a bed and breakfast. He mentioned a bed and breakfast. What was the name? I thought it was funny because I'm from New York—the York! He's staying at the York Bed and Breakfast!"

Dropping the phone, Royce rushed to Miriam's computer in the front room to look it up.

13

"If he won't pick up my calls, I'll just have to corner him and *make* him talk to me," Royce muttered. She brought up a search engine on the computer to look up the York Bed & Breakfast in Fort Worth. Scanning its home page, she murmured, "That's a lovely place. He must be doing well to afford that."

Noting the phone number, she retrieved her phone from the tea table and dialed. It was almost a relief to hear a live voice on the other end answer, "York Bed and Breakfast. This is Sharon."

Royce cleared her throat. "Hello. I'm looking for Paul Arrendondo. Can you tell me what room he's in, please?"

"Oh, Mr. Arrendondo checked out—yesterday morning? Yes, I think it was yesterday."

Royce's heart sank. "Do you know where he went?"

"No, I'm sorry, I don't."

"All right. Thank you." Royce quietly put the phone in her purse, then went to the tiny bedroom to stretch across her bed and burst into tears. "Oh, I screwed up so bad here. What was I thinking? I can't believe he came after me and I just threw him away like that. Now he's really, truly gone, and I—"

She stopped crying and sat up. "He said he'd applied to a Streiker company here in town. It was the . . . ?"

Paul sat at the desk, playing with a string of cheese from his third piece of pizza. *Who is doing this? Who's equipping this place for me to live here? Somebody's taking my notes and acting on them—except for a phone. I need a phone.*

He put down the pizza, wiped his hands, and extracted all cash from his wallet to count it. Over $500. Without a credit card, surely that was enough to secure service on another phone, especially if he reported his old one stolen, which it certainly was.

Why would they put a refrigerator in here but not give me a phone? Or even answer my request for another interview? Since this was all so vexing, Paul leaned back to the refrigerator to pull out a bottle of beer.

He unscrewed the top and took a swig, thinking. Baby's Cantina? *I think I know where that is.* It'd be a nice diversion, to sit around with the guys over a beer, maybe meet some girls. *Yeah, I might do that.* None of those guys helped him much at work, but, they might be better company drunk. *Heck, forget them. I'll just go meet a new girl.* He took another swig, looking down at the tattered athletic shoes he wore. *Better change those.* His boots looked better. Girls liked nice boots.

So he pulled off his shoes and socks, staring down at his bare feet. *My boots are over there*, he directed himself, looking at his boots. *They're dirty. They really need cleaning.* But the leather cleaner he had left at Jeannine's, and he didn't really feel like cleaning his boots anyway. He was awfully tired. *But they need it. I can't go someplace to meet girls looking like I do manual work for a living.*

His mind's eye called up the image of a pretty girl he had glimpsed at the mall, and he smiled. He envisioned her at Baby's Cantina. And there he is, approaching her in his nice, clean boots. She looks up and smiles; he sits down to chat. She watches him, hanging on his every word while he describes robbing drug runners in Big Bend.

He buys her a drink; she touches his hand when he gives it to her. Then he leans in for a kiss—not too aggressive, now. She closes her eyes to respond—

But from there, the scenario kicked into fast forward. A little dumbfounded at no longer being in control of this fantasy, Paul watched her wrap him around her little finger while he promises undying devotion. There is a little exhilarating sex, then she gets angry, rips him into shreds, and walks out. Thus ends his marriage with nameless #3.

So he stood up from the desk, but instead of picking up his boots, he picked up his book. Since he had it in his hand, he sat on the bed, plumping the pillow behind his back, and opened it to resume reading of Aeneas' visit to the underworld, the place of the dead:

Before the entrance, in the jaws of Orcus,
Grief and avenging Cares have made their beds,
And pale Diseases and sad Age are there,
And Dread, and Hunger that sways men to crime,

And sordid Want—in shapes to affright the eyes—
And Death and Toil and Death's own brother, Sleep,
And the mind's evil joys; on the door sill
Death-bringing War, and iron cubicles
Of the Eumenidës, and raving Discord,
Viperish hair bound up in gory bands.
In the courtyard a shadowy giant elm
Spreads ancient boughs, her ancient arms where dreams,
False dreams, the old tale goes, beneath each leaf
Cling and are numberless. There, too,
About the doorway forms of monsters crowd—
Centaurs, twiformed Scyllas, hundred-armed
Briareus, and the Lernaean hydra
Hissing horribly, and the Chimaera
Breathing dangerous flames, and Gorgons, Harpies,
Huge Geryon, triple-bodied ghost.
Here, swept by sudden fear, drawing his sword,
Aeneas stood on guard with naked edge
Against them as they came. If his companion,
Knowing the truth, had not admonished him
How faint these lives were—empty images
Hovering bodiless—he had attacked
And cut his way through phantoms, empty air.

Paul suddenly stopped reading, looking up at the voiceless question: Why had he not finished this book years ago? What had he been so afraid of?

He looked down at the page without seeing it. At the time, he thought he was about to discover that he shouldn't go to seminary, which course was already set in stone. But now he saw that wasn't it at all—going to seminary wasn't a mistake; he proved that by getting the degree. His father was correct, in seeing his son's abilities better than he himself did.

Paul's mistake lay in not questioning his fears, not facing them. Had he confronted his terrors head on, as Aeneas did, he would have discovered them to be nothing more than ghosts, shadows. And he would have saved himself years of self-blame.

At once disturbed and encouraged by this discovery, he returned to the book to find out more about himself. Fully engaged in the story, Paul forgot all about Baby's Cantina. Harrison, Bauhaus, even Royce gave way to Aeneas on his quest to speak with his beloved dead father.

With Miriam still gone, Royce sat at her computer, drumming her fingers, staring at the blank screen. She moved the mouse to bring up Miriam's home page, then sat there until the screen went blank again. Her intent was to locate the company Paul had applied to work for. But what she thought about was her telling him how she needed to be independent.

That's right; I should be, she mused. *I should be able to support myself. But I should have made that decision before we got married. I can't just change the rules on him like that.* She sucked in a breath. *Okay. That's one of the things I'll explain when I talk to him.*

To encourage herself, she talked out loud: "He said he was applying to a Streiker company in town. He must have gotten the job; that must be why he left the bed and breakfast, because it was just temporary. The name of the company was. . . ."

All the concentrated thought she could muster did not produce the name. She exhaled, "It was such a strange name! Foreign-sounding. Occupina something. Occupina presentium. Occulina credintium. Offintina derentium. Does any of that sound right? No."

Bringing up the browser window again, she entered "Streiker companies Fort Worth" in the search engine field and began clicking on results. But none of them looked remotely like the name she was looking for, so she revised her search terms three or four times and continued looking.

Forty minutes later, she gave up and closed the window. "Well, that's that," she said. "I can't remember it, and he's not calling me back, so I'll just forget him and go on. I mean, that's what I intended when I left the ranch, right?"

No, she realized. What she had intended was for Paul to do just what he did: leave the ranch and come looking for her. She wanted him to demonstrate that she meant more to him than the Ferrings did.

But Paul didn't think in those terms. He had a very linear way of thinking: one thing at a time. He felt obligated to the Ferrings, so he stayed put when she left. Since he didn't come after her right away, by the time he did show up, she felt the need to punish him a little, make him wait in the wings for her to decide to take him back.

All the while, in the back of her mind, she knew that eventually she *would* take him back. She wasn't so stupid as to refuse someone who loved her that much. But Paul, with his literal, linear mindset, interpreted her dallying as a point-blank refusal and . . . left.

"I really wish I hadn't done that now," she murmured. Well, repentance was great, except that it was too late. She thought back to when she had left Buddy and Renetta's wedding with Perry a year ago June. When she discovered that Perry was taking her to Big Bend instead of Fort Worth, she thought it was too late. But she had closed her eyes in the blinding afternoon light and whispered a prayer to Padre, the God she had ignored most of her life.

And He had answered. But when she was returned to Paul, and they were married, and settled into life on the ranch, she had forgotten Him again—until now. Wasn't it presumptuous to think she could keep Him in a box like a genie, to help her whenever she got into trouble and not bother her otherwise?

"Padre, please help me find him," she whispered, "and I won't ignore You anymore. Even if he doesn't want me."

Paul read late into the night; he had no idea what time it was when he finally reached up to turn off the reading light. Unknown hours later, he was awakened—again—by the pounding on the far door. "I'm coming!" he called, reaching up blindly for the light.

Groaning, he rolled out of bed, swiping at his athletic shoes on the floor. When he had sufficiently pulled himself together (not bothering to shave), he stuffed the key into his back pocket and trotted to the door.

He was a little surprised, upon emerging, not to see Cam waiting for him, but decided that Cam knew by now he'd come. With all his worldly possessions in the warehouse, he took care to lock the door. Then he hustled over to Bauhaus.

First thing upon arriving, he helped himself to the breakfast spread and used the rest room in the back of the warehouse. (It smelled *bad* back here—worse than his truck ever did.) Emerging from the warehouse, he looked into the lit bay where the customers' trucks were already lining up. To his surprise, he saw Cam handing out numbers to the drivers. Paul hurried over to see what was going on.

Eyes bloodshot, Cam glanced at Paul's approach. "Well, here you are. Again. Trying to make a point about how righteous you are?"

"What?" Paul said, flabbergasted.

"Oh, working so hard to make everybody else look bad, so now Seth is jumping all down my throat. By the way, didn't see you last night at Baby's," Cam said, walking to another driver to hand him his number. Cam (or Seth) had found nice plastic numbers for the drivers, instead of the improvisational marker Paul had been using.

"Mark 'number 4' on my sheet," the driver reminded him. Irritably, Cam stopped to scribble "4" on that order and move on, looking hugely hung over.

Paul moved with him. "Last night? . . . Oh, I meant to come, but I was so tired I just crashed. Sorry about that."

"Well," Cam said, handing another customer a number, "we don't need as many guys today, but I guess I can find something for you to do."

Paul stared at him. "Didn't you come knock on the warehouse door just now?"

"No," Cam said, scrawling on an order sheet the number he'd just given one driver. "Like I said, we've got it covered today."

Paul stood by, watching, as the semi arrived and parked. Then Cam began distributing orders according to the system Paul had created yesterday.

When Paul saw a driver who had no assistant but three containers to load, he hurried over to help him. Only two other Bauhaus crewmen were on the job today, and they were all that was needed to fill the orders. Despite the heavy Saturday demand, the loading still progressed faster than it had Wednesday, Paul's first day here. And all he did was move containers.

Miriam got home just in time that morning to take Royce to work. "I'm sorry for the inconvenience of driving me everywhere," Royce murmured, climbing into the passenger seat while the engine idled roughly.

"Oh, no bother," Miriam waved. She was so giggly, disheveled, and breathless that Royce almost didn't trust her to drive. "I needed an excuse to rush out—don't want to seem clingy at this point." Upon exiting the apartment parking lot, Miriam whipped around corners and blatantly ran a red light to avoid stopping, as the car showed a new tendency to stall out.

Royce gripped the armrest. "You must've had a great time."

"Oh, it was so—oh, here you are." Miriam slammed on the brakes to turn into the bookstore's parking lot, having arrived in record time. "Hope you're not late. We'll talk when you get off tonight."

She pulled up to the front walk, almost running over

it, and Royce opened the car door, saying, "Okay. Thanks so much. See you tonight." Miriam blew her a kiss as Royce closed the door.

Then, despondently, she went on into the bookstore. She was glad for Miriam, but saw too clearly the handwriting on the wall: she was about to lose her roommate and her transportation.

She knew it wouldn't last—it was too coincidental how, when she had stepped off the bus from San Angelo, she had met Miriam waiting to pick up a friend who never showed. When Miriam had taken pity on her, driving her to the Phoenix Street Center, offering her a place to stay while she got on her feet at the bookstore— even then Royce knew it was meant to be temporary . . . until Paul came for her.

It being Saturday, the store was very busy—Royce had little time to brood over her situation. Therefore, she was glad for the diversion of helping customers find what they were looking for. Most were interested in books, obviously, having come to a bookstore. But they came with the oddest questions that, by some quirk of fate, she knew how to answer.

She happened to hear one male customer vent to another, "This is stupid. I'm never gonna find anything here."

So she stepped within view to say, "Tell me what you need. If we don't have it, I can let you know right away."

He looked her over skeptically, but said, "My uncle bought a farm and thinks he's gonna raise cattle, but he don't know the first thing about—"

"Over here," Royce nodded.

She took him across the store and pulled a book from a shelf. "This is the authority on raising beef cattle. I know of experienced ranchers who carry it around with them everywhere."

His friend, looking over his shoulder, exclaimed, "Storey! That's it! That's the one I was trying to think of."

The shopper eyed her in surprise, then shut his mouth and took the book to the check-out counter.

Royce began reshelving books that had been left lying around, and one woman tentatively approached her. "Excuse me?"

"Yes?" Royce turned, smiling.

"I . . . hope you don't mind. I love your shoes. Such a cute casual. They look comfortable, too. Can you tell me where you got them?" the woman asked.

In a flash Royce remembered that purchase. She bought them on impulse with the debit card for her and Paul's joint account even though she knew he was buying parts to repair the truck that day. The simultaneous debits caused their account to be overdrawn, and the bank called Jeannine. She made up the difference without a word to anyone. Royce only found out about it much later. "They're Paige by Lazio. You can get them online," Royce said.

The woman's face fell slightly. "They must be expensive."

"A little," Royce admitted. Taking stock of the woman's helpless envy, she added, "Have you got some paper?"

Hesitantly, the woman pulled a scrap piece and pen from her purse, and Royce wrote down a website address. "This is the website of a garment wholesaler I know in New York. His name is Lowell Lindel. Tell him Royce asked him to give you a good deal, and he will."

The customer took the paper dubiously, glancing at "Royce" on her nametag. "Are you sure?"

"Yes." Royce bit her lip, smiling.

"Okay. Thanks." Her shopping done, the woman exited the store.

At that point, Royce noticed one woman staring dolefully at the books on a shelf in the children's section. So she went over to ask, "Can I help you find something?"

"I doubt it. I'm looking for a particular book I read as a child, but I don't remember the title or who wrote it," the customer replied. "I just remember how I felt when I read it. It was such a wonderful book about things that were blown away by the wind being kept in a magic attic—"

"The handkerchief you forgot to hold,
The spelling paper with the star of gold,
The picture you drew for Mother's Day,
All the things you somehow let drift away
Aren't exactly lost. So before you cry—
Why not look in the Attic in the sky?"

Royce quoted. Although she continued to smile, tears came to her eyes.

"That's it!" the woman exclaimed, staring at her. "How did you know?"

Blinking rapidly, Royce bent to scan the lower shelves, where the tall books were kept. "I worked at a children's book publisher in New York, and you happen to be looking for a classic. It's called *Attic of the Wind* by Doris Herold Lund—oh, here it is! I didn't know we had it." She pulled a large, slender hardback off the shelf to hand to the customer.

"This is it," the woman breathed, running her hand over the cover. "I have a new granddaughter, and I want to read it to her. I can't believe you knew what I was looking for. Thank you."

"You're welcome," Royce said, smiling gamely.

While the woman took the book to the check-out counter, Royce took a ten-minute break to close herself in the rest room with her phone. "If anybody's got an attic, The Streiker Corporation does," she muttered. She scrolled through the numbers stored on her phone—she knew she had it in here somewhere. "Ah. There it is." She dialed and put the phone to her ear.

"Thank you for calling The Streiker Corporation. We would like to hear from you, so please call back during our office hours, which are eight A.M. to five P.M. Monday through Friday." There was a momentary lull in the recording, and Royce almost put the phone away. Then she heard, "If your call is urgent, our after-hours number is . . . do you have a pen?"

"No, but I'll store it in my phone," Royce replied. Her eyes glazed over at the realization that she was talking to a recording, but then she heard the number being given. Repeating it to herself over and over, she took the phone from her ear to enter the digits in storage. Then she dialed.

Nervous, she put the phone to her ear again and waited. "Hello?" a woman answered—a live one.

Royce cleared her throat. "Hello, my name is Royce Arrendondo. I work at the Old Book Shoppe. Um, my husband Paul came looking for me, and I lost touch with him, and I really need to get hold of him. He told me he's working for one of the Streiker companies here in Fort Worth, but I can't remember the name. It was a very odd name. Can you—please tell me where he's working so I can get hold of him?"

"I'll pass along the message," the woman said.

Is that all? Royce sagged. "You . . . couldn't . . . look it up for me, real quick?" she pleaded.

"No, I'm sorry; I've not been authorized to do that."

"I understand. But you'll pass along the message?" Royce asked.

"Yes, I certainly will."

"Okay, well, thank you."

"You're welcome," the Streiker employee replied.

Blinking back tears, Royce put her phone away and returned to work. But then she wondered, *Who's she going to pass the message along to? Paul? What good would that do, when he wouldn't take my calls?* Pondering this, she set herself to stocking shelves.

Since Cam had commandeered the position in the refrigerated semi, Paul was left to haul containers to the multistop trucks waiting in the sun. Today was really hot, as was every other day in Texas between May and October. Paul took a thirty-second break to help himself to the bottled waters from the rack, but other than that, kept at it until all waiting trucks had received their orders. He did not notice the three or four times that Seth came out of his office to watch the unloading.

Then, soaked with sweat, Paul collapsed in the shade and rested his head on his knees, too drained to even get up for more water. Day after day of this was really starting to wear him down. A few minutes later Cam came over to chide jokingly, "You think you're going to get paid for lounging around all day?"

Paul raised his head to squint at him. *I've been doing ten times the work you have, moron, and I've got a master's degree. Did you even graduate high school?* The temptation to air just a fraction of the insults that roiled his brain was almost overpowering. But as a matter of practicality, Paul swallowed the contention. Slowly, he got to his feet. "Okay. We got a clogged drain that needs cleaning," Cam said.

Whereupon he took Paul to the rear of the warehouse, where a six-inch drain cover had been removed from its place in the floor. Here, at last, was the origin of the awful smell. Kneeling to peer down in the hole, Paul saw murky water standing. "Have at it," Cam said, smiling.

Paul rocked back on his heels to look up at him, and Cam waited for the refusal that was so evidently coming. Paul would tell him to go soak his head, then Cam could go report to Seth that the Hero Worker had wimped out on them. But when Paul opened his mouth to fulfill Cam's expectations, he saw—no, *felt*—the presence of Aeneas, almost as if he were inside him. As if they were one and the same.

Standing in the strength of his supernatural heritage, Paul said, "I'll need a snake and some rubber gloves."

"Utility closet's over there," Cam nodded before walking off.

Paul ransacked the storage closet for the needed items. He donned the heavy gloves, then knelt over the drain to begin running the auger-headed coil through the obstruction.

Slowly, painfully, with repeated insertions and withdrawals, the head on the snake brought up bits and pieces of mostly unidentifiable debris—decomposing seafood, grass, hair, dirt—that Paul deposited into a trash sack by the handfuls.

All the while, he was Aeneas. This rotting thatch that he pulled from the drain had been left there by the Eumenidës, the goddesses of punishment who had snake hair and blood-dripping eyes. They thought to dismay him with their refuse, but he cleared it away and pressed on.

The next bit of blackened gunk was obviously the excrement of the Harpies—birdlike creatures with the long, pale faces of women ravaged by hunger. Paul fought his way through them only to come upon the hydra: the many-headed snake whose breath was so poisonous, it would kill any mortal who approached even when it was sleeping. Undaunted, Paul extracted the mass to bury it in his trash bag.

Last, and worst of all, he came upon the Chimaera—the fire-breathing monster, part lion, part goat, part snake, which in this case had arranged its parts to resemble a decomposing, very dead rat. This Paul vanquished only by means of great courage and the skillful use of his weapon.

After three hours of heroic labor, when the plumbing snake brought up nothing else, Paul poured industrial-strength drain cleaner into the opening, chasing it with a fierce stream from the water hose for about ten minutes. As the drain appeared to be clear, he spent another thirty minutes locating a drain filter that actually fit, and putting that in place.

By then it was three o'clock. Paul looked at the vestiges of barbecue left out on the table, but there wasn't even enough for a sandwich. No matter; after that last job, he didn't have much appetite. So he went looking for Cam. Not finding him, he settled for Seth, who was working at the desk in his office. When Paul leaned on the door frame, Seth looked up. "Ah, the drain's clear," Paul reported.

Seth put down his pen, regarding him, then reached for a side drawer. "Paul, you're a terrific worker. I really appreciate your attitude. You've shown everybody here what it means to work. We're closed tomorrow, but we'll see you on Monday. Thank you." And Seth handed him a wad of bills.

Blinking, Paul looked through the cash: five hundred dollars. All he could muster was a raised brow and, "Okay." Then he dragged himself back to his warehouse home next door.

Pulling out his key—his proof of legitimate occupancy—he unlocked the door and entered, eager to see what surprises awaited him. But nothing was different; even the pizza he'd left out last night was still out—which was really kind of stupid, considering that he had a refrigerator to put it in. But, no phone. Then it crossed his mind that he hadn't left a note this morning.

In a haze of exhaustion, Paul showered and changed. As he ate some more pizza (washed down with a nice cold beer) he pulled out all his cash and counted it: one thousand fifteen dollars. He stacked the bills in a neat pile. With this much he could definitely get another phone, and leave a note for Harrison to call him. . . .

He looked across the vacant space of the warehouse, apprehending that a phone was not his top priority right now. Obviously, he was communicating just fine with Harrison—or someone—who was taking his needs seriously. There was something else that must be done with this cash.

In groaning reluctance, Paul climbed into his truck and drove to a convenience store. He exchanged $1000 of his cash for money orders made out to Jeannine Ferring. Then he bought a prestamped envelope, bummed paper from the clerk, and composed this note:

Dear Jeannine:

I found Royce. She's doing fine, but is not interested in getting back together. But I found a really cheap place to live and a job. It's [here he struggled a little with the wording] not what I'd most like to do for a living, but it pays well enough. My credit-card statements will be coming to your house soon. Together, they've got over $7000 on them. Please use this $1000 to make a payment, and I will send more as I earn it. I will also send some for your boarding Mama, if you don't mind keeping her there a little while longer. [He couldn't see bringing her to the warehouse to live.]

I lost my phone, so can't call, but will get another ASAP. Hope you are well. Please share this with Buddy when you hear from him.

Thanks,
Paul

He sealed up the note in the envelope with the money orders, addressed it to Jeannine, and dropped it in the mailbox. With $3 of his last $15, he bought ranch dip to go with his leftover pizza, and so returned to the warehouse.

Miriam was much more composed when she picked up Royce from the bookstore that evening. "How was work? Did you have a good day?" she asked solicitously.

"Yes, thank you, it was all right," Royce replied.

"Oh, look, here's a Taco Bell coming up. Is that okay for dinner tonight?" Miriam asked, turning the wheel into the drive-through lane.

"Sure," Royce said, reaching for her purse.

"No, no—I'll pay," Miriam insisted.

"You don't have to do that," Royce said, mildly alarmed.

"No, really, I insist. What would you like?" Miriam pulled up to the menu.

"Ah, the nachos look good," Royce said, with a bare glance at the menu.

"Yes, they do." Miriam gave their order over the intercom, then pulled on up to the window to pay. "Gosh, I need gas again. My mileage is terrible all of a sudden."

"You really don't have to buy me dinner," Royce said, a trifle anxious.

"Well, I'd feel better if I did," Miriam confessed.

"Why?" Royce asked.

"Honey, we have to talk."

14

Here it comes, Royce thought with a sinking feeling. "What's on your mind?"

"Let's get the food home and eat," Miriam said.

So they took the sacks back to the apartment. Royce unlocked the door, and they unloaded their dinner on the tea table. While they settled down to eat, Royce made a preemptive strike: "Miriam, I can't tell you how much I appreciate everything you've done for me since I moved here. I never expected you to take care of me forever. If you need me to move out, or get my own transportation, I'd just have to say it's about time."

Miriam exhaled, "Oh, you don't know how glad I am to hear that! But you don't need to move out—I just wanted to let you know that probably within the next two weeks *I'll* be moving out. My doctor popped the question," she said coyly.

"Miriam! He asked you to marry him?" Royce gasped.

"Yes. We're going shopping for rings tonight."

"Miriam!" Royce squealed, jumping up to squeeze her around the shoulders. "I am so happy for you!"

"Thank you," Miriam patted her arms. "I'm so relieved you feel that way! I was just afraid—I mean, sometimes when your own marriage isn't happy—I mean—"

"No, really, Miriam; I'm sure you will be very happy. It was my own fault things didn't work out with Paul, and if I had another chance to have him back, I would in a heartbeat," Royce said.

"He seemed like a nice guy. He was certainly nice looking," Miriam said tentatively.

"And easy to take for granted," Royce said. She paused to make sure no tears would be allowed to spoil Miriam's news.

"Well, even if things don't work out between you and Paul, I'm not stranding you," Miriam said firmly. "I talked to one of Doctor Bear's nurses who needs a place to stay, and she's coming to room with you. She has a nicer car than mine, and she said she'd be thrilled to drive you places in exchange for gas and maintenance. Her name is Carole, and she is a sweetheart. Very clean, easygoing, not a party girl. She's a Baptist."

"Well, no one could be as lovely as you, but I'm sure we'll get along fine. Thank you for thinking of me," Royce murmured, downcast. She didn't want *Carole*, she wanted *Paul*.

"There's just one tiny little problem." Miriam puckered her lips, implying that it was a *funny* tiny little problem.

"What?" Royce asked, brows raised.

"She's a huge country and western fan!" Miriam screeched.

Royce laughed loudly at the joke. Inside she was

ranting, *Country* and *Western? HUGE? Are you kidding me? No. NO. Paul, where are you?* Winding down the laughter, Royce changed the subject: "So tell me everything about your doctor!"

"*Well*—" Miriam began talking, and Royce made herself listen to every word.

Paul cleared away his pizza trash and kicked off his shoes to sit up in bed with his book. He was fairly sure that Cam and the crew would be partying at Baby's Cantina tonight, but Paul had zero desire to join them, girls or no girls. Since he had tomorrow off, he intended to read as long as it suited him. Opening the book, once more he was with Aeneas

> And mowed the Latins down. He killed the giant
> Theron, who left ranks to encounter him,
> Bent on meeting the enemy champion.
> A sword-blade driven through his bronze chain-mail
> And tunic stiff with gold drank from his side
> Slashed open. . . .

Hours later, the warring stayed with Paul as the book finally fell from his limp fingers. Images of blood, and fire, and the shades of the underworld mingled incoherently in his dreams, until finally he opened his eyes. For a heart-stopping moment, he thought he was lying slain on the battlefield himself, for flickering orange lights danced in his peripheral vision.

As he came to, sitting up, he realized that those orange lights had wakened him. He smelled smoke. He looked up in sudden alarm to the windows on the side of the warehouse that faced Bauhaus, and saw the unmistakable light of dancing flames.

Paul scrambled out of bed and ran to the front door, barefoot and keyless. Barreling outside, he raced next door to see flames leaping from the rear of the Bauhaus warehouse. "Sh—!" he cried. He glimpsed the security guard's car, but not the man himself anywhere.

Paul spread his hands in urgent frustration. "I've got NO PHONE!" And the sprinkler system was not even completely installed yet. While he was standing stricken in the street, his attention seized on three figures emerging from Bauhaus' front door, laughing and whooping. "Hey!" Paul shouted angrily. "Hey, you!"

They jumped, then started running away. Paul glimpsed their shaved heads and chains, but was too pumped with adrenalin to hesitate: he ran right after them. The middle guy was the slowest, being drunk or stoned. Paul caught him by the choke chain around his neck and brought him down, falling on top of him on the concrete drive.

The other two turned back to assist their buddy. One grabbed Paul's arm and punched him repeatedly in the face until his grip on the guy loosened, then the second kicked Paul in the chest, sending him sprawling back onto the drive.

They hauled up their injured friend and hustled him off between them while Paul sat up, clutching at the pain in his back. Wiping blood from his mouth, he watched them disappear into the night. Then he looked back toward the burning warehouse—it would be a total loss if he didn't summon help immediately. The fire would probably spread to the Officina warehouse next door.

Paul staggered to his feet, taking deep breaths as he trotted toward the jimmied door. Then he held his breath and wrenched open the door to run inside.

The smoke and the darkness blinded him at once, but he knew exactly where the nearest fire alarm was—he had leaned against it more than once. Arms outstretched, he stumbled forward till he encountered the column and ran his hands along it. Finding the alarm, he yanked it, then turned back for the door.

He found the front wall, but had to grope along it searching for the door. His eyes were watering fiercely, and he was soon forced to cough, expelling precious breath. But at last he fell on the door and shoved it open.

Gasping, coughing, and retching, he stumbled blindly away from the building until he ran into the security guard's car. Paul leaned on it, sucking in deep breaths. Even the air outside the warehouse was hot and smoky, so it took a while for his head to clear. At last he opened his stinging eyes. The first thing he saw was the guard asleep in the front seat, tilted far back for comfort.

"You f—— a———! Wake up, you ———!" With a string of furious expletives, Paul beat on the car, rocking it violently. He tried to open the door, but it was locked. The guard startled up, blinking at him. Prudently, he made no move to exit with a raving lunatic thrashing around his car.

Sirens. Paul exhaled in relief, seeing the fire truck career around the corner, a couple of police cars in tow. He stepped back out of the way to watch the firefighters leap off the truck and pull out hoses.

A police officer approached him, shining a flashlight in his eyes. "Hey, pal. What do you know about this?"

Winded, Paul was collecting himself to reply when the security guard behind him said, "He set the fire and attacked me!"

Paul turned to sarcastically congratulate him for finally getting out of his vehicle when the cop shoved him face first onto the cruiser, ordering, "Hands on the hood! Spread your legs!"

Paul complied at once, but said calmly, "He was sleeping in his car. There were three punks in the building—they ran off when I hollered at them. I ran inside to pull the fire alarm—"

"Uh huh," the officer said, handcuffing his wrists behind his back. Although Paul's compliance calmed him somewhat, he wasn't listening to the suspect's explanation, seeing how obviously guilty he was. He patted Paul's pockets, which were all empty. "What's your name? You got an ID?"

"My name is Paul Arrendondo. My wallet's in the warehouse next door," Paul nodded over his shoulder. "I interviewed for a job there, and I've been sleeping there."

"Okay, Paul; have a seat and we'll check it out." The officer steered him by the shoulder to sit in the back seat of the cruiser. Paul sat, watching as the security guard threw back his shoulders and straightened his belt to report to the officers arriving on the scene. While Paul was detained as perpetrator, the newly courageous security guard gave the cops his completely fabricated version of events.

Paul leaned over to the window to listen: "Ah, yeah, I'm making my rounds, and this guy came out and jumped me—"

"From where?" one cop asked.

"Well, he was in the building, and—"

"How did he get in?" another cop asked.

"I'm not real sure—I think he broke a window in back. When I saw the first signs of smoke, I started running back there. He jumped out and hit me. I wrestled him to the ground, but he got away from me, and then you guys showed," the guard said, panting as if he'd been in a fight.

"Okay, come show me where this happened," a sergeant gestured, and the security guard accompanied him around the building.

Another fire truck arrived to tackle the blaze from the side of the building. Meanwhile, Paul listened to the officers by the cruiser talk, looking over to the warehouse next door. One must have mentioned Paul's claim to tenancy in the warehouse, for another said, "That building's been vacant for years."

A third cop said, "I'll go have a look," and sprinted toward it with a high-powered flashlight.

At that time, it crossed Paul's mind that he had no proof of anything. He had nothing in writing to confirm that he had interviewed there, or that he had anyone's permission to stay there. He had met Vince Harrison exactly once, had no way of getting hold of him now—and, for that matter, did not even know that Harrison himself was actually in the employ of The Streiker Corporation.

Paul craned his neck to keep sight of the investigating officer, whose shadowy figure approached the door. It must have been locked, for he began going around the building, and Paul lost him in the darkness.

In a while, however, the cop returned. Paul leaned against the window to listen as he told his fellow officer, "The building's secure. All doors locked; no windows broken, no evidence of any tampering. He got any key on him, or anything?"

"Nope," the other said, glancing toward the suspect.

Another noted, "Security says he's just a vagrant."

"Okay, then, run him in."

Whereupon the officer and his partner sat in the front seat of the patrol car. The first turned to Paul behind the wire screen. "Okay, you're under arrest for suspicion of arson. You have the right to remain silent. Anything you say can and will be used against you in a court of law. You have the right to talk to a lawyer and have him present with you while you are being questioned. If you cannot afford to hire a lawyer, one will be appointed to represent you before you answer any questions. Do you understand these rights?"

"Yes," Paul said, sitting back.

So the cop started the car, making a radio call. Then he drove Paul a few blocks to the main police station, where he was unloaded.

Being late Saturday night (actually, early Sunday morning) the station house was busy. Paul had to wait in line to get searched and booked. After he was photographed and fingerprinted, he was taken before a tired, overworked sergeant who glanced at him disparagingly. "No identification. You another illegal? *Se habla* English?"

Paul's face burned. "Yes. I am an American citizen by birth."

"Yeah, well, you do us proud. Arson's a state jail

felony, so you post bail tonight or you're off to Hutchins in the morning. Bail's set at five thousand dollars. Anybody you want to call? You get one phone call."

Who to call? Who would vouch for him? Seth? Royce? Mr. Streiker? Paul swallowed. "No, no one."

The sergeant nodded at a bailiff. "Okay, take him to holding. Next!"

Paul was escorted to a large holding cell and uncuffed. It was crowded with about thirty patrons, most of them sleepy drunks, a few belligerent drunks. The benches were taken, so Paul sat on the floor. A few of the shades in this underworld roused in interest upon his arrival. One asked, "What're you in for?"

"Being in the wrong place at the wrong time," Paul replied.

"Weren't we all," the other snorted.

Paul didn't care to say any more, but let the heckling and arguing flow around him. Leaning his head back against the wall, he thought, *Well, there goes the job with Officina Gentium—if there really was any such thing. And at Bauhaus, for that matter. Oh, well. I was tired of hauling boxes. I won't want any seafood again for a while, that's for sure. But they probably don't serve fresh seafood in state jail, anyway. Where did he say? Hutchins. That's in Dallas.*

When two detainees initiated a fight beside him, he scooted out of their way and continued to think over the events of the last month. Let's see: he'd lost Royce, then Walt, then five grand trying to resuscitate a dead man.

He'd walked away from a cushy situation keeping Jeannine company. He chased some phantom job for a phantom billionaire, and got himself arrested for trying to save Bauhaus' building and inventory. And almost every penny he had, he'd sent to Jeannine as payment on his credit-card debt, but that was okay, because that paltry thousand would have covered only one-fifth of his bail, anyway.

So did he have anything to complain about now? All down the line, he had done the best he could do—the right thing as far as he was able. To the best of his ability, in his circumstances, he had been Aeneas. So let the gods—God—do to him as He would.

Paul watched an inmate throw up, and another sob in maudlin drunkenness, and wondered if he'd be able to find another copy of *The Aeneid* in the state jail library. Also, he'd lose his truck. Once they figured out he had been squatting in Streiker's warehouse, they'd impound his truck, and by the time he got out, impound fees would exceed the value of the vehicle.

Now, that thought hurt. As he looked around at his sweaty, stinking, peeing cell mates, the reality of his situation closed in on him. There was no way he could prove that he didn't set that fire. From any objective angle, he looked guilty. What was his motive? Why, he had to work there for four days. Anybody would want to torch the place after having to clean a dead rat out of the drain. He was in trouble, and he was going to jail.

How pathetic was it now that he had been imagining himself to be Aeneas?—a fictional character in a fictional work—old and venerated, but still make-believe.

I've been living in make-believe, Paul thought. The black-clad biker beside him roused from a stupor to take a swing at him, so he scooted away to let him whop up on somebody else.

It was all make-believe—thinking I could get Royce back, or that a billionaire would take an interest in me, or that I'm anything other than a failed preacher with a useless education. This is reality, he thought. *Concrete floor, iron bars, and ten-to-twenty for arson.*

By now, he was secure in the bitter satisfaction of having it all figured out: the deck had been stacked against him from the beginning. The idea that he could change anything about his destiny was fantasy. As usual, the gods had won.

So he waited, indifferently watching another fight, until weariness closed his eyes.

"Royce." Having dressed for the morning, Miriam was sitting at her computer, going through her mail and such. "Royce?"

"Be right there!" Royce called from the bedroom. She was doing something that shamed her deeply, and she didn't want to get caught. But she couldn't help it.

After Miriam had come in last night to show off the engagement ring that she and her Doctor Bear had picked out, Royce admired it with all appropriate exclamations. But deep in her heart, she suspected something. She burned all night to prove or disprove her suspicions, but never had a chance until this morning, when Miriam had gotten ready and left the bedroom without it. Now was Royce's chance.

She dug in her own lingerie drawer to bring out a ring box hidden in the back. Opening it, she looked at the diamond ring Paul had bought for her. Then she placed Miriam's new diamond ring next to it, to compare them. As she suspected, the ranch hand's diamond was bigger, with more fire and brilliance, than the doctor's. Paul had spent every dime he had to buy her the best diamond he could find in San Angelo.

"Royce?"

"Coming!" she called, blinking.

Hastily replacing the ring box, she found something else that she had stolen from Paul and brought up here to hide. With constricted heart, she brought out the old photograph of Paul's great-grandfather, the circuit rider. Staring at the handsome man on horseback, Royce suddenly knew why she took it when she left: she loved him. She loved both the preacher she never knew, and the preacher she had married. Her absconding with this photo was her way of guaranteeing that Paul would come for her.

"Royce!"

Throwing her things back into the drawer, Royce shut it and came out with a breathless, happy air. "I'm sorry! I was admiring your ring again! When is your doctor coming to pick you up?"

She handed the ring to Miriam, who absently put it on. "Nine o'clock. In about thirty minutes," Miriam said, glancing at the computer's clock.

"That's great. I'm so relieved he's going to take your car in for that tune-up. Oh, Miriam, I'm so happy for you. Your diamond is gorgeous. Listen, you don't have to worry about getting me to work today," she chatted, having already decided to walk. It was only about two miles.

"That's fine, but I thought you'd better look at this news item," Miriam said.

"What is it?" Royce asked, disinterested.

"Your husband's been arrested," Miriam said.

"What?" Royce gasped. "Paul? Arrested?"

"Yes—for arson, it says. Isn't that him?" She sat back from the computer for Royce to look at the monitor. There was a mug shot of a weary-looking Paul with a swollen lip.

"I don't believe it," Royce breathed.

"Yeah, that's rough. His bail is five thousand dollars," Miriam noted sympathetically. "And they're transporting him to the state jail in Dallas today."

"I don't believe it—" Royce suddenly ran to the other room to snatch up her phone. She keyed an entry with trembling fingers, then put the phone to her ear, whispering, "Please answer, please answer—" Then: "Daddy! I need five thousand dollars right away!"

"Arrendondo! Paul Arrendondo!"

Starting awake, Paul pulled himself up from the cement floor of the cell with a groan. He shuffled to the door, which was unlocked by the officer on duty. "You have visitors." The cop nodded down the hall.

Rubbing his stiff neck, Paul accompanied him down that hall, through the steel-reinforced door, and around the corner to the outer office of the detention facility. There, his heart sank to see a solemn Seth, standing with someone else in a coat and tie.

Drawing up to the two, Paul took a breath, then looked his employer in the eye to say, "I didn't set the fire, Seth."

"I know, Paul," he nodded.

The other man said, "Okay, Arrendondo, you're free to go."

Paul blinked at him. "Who are you?"

"Detective Claussen, Gang Unit. We just finished reviewing the surveillance tape. It shows everything pretty clearly, except the faces of the gang members. Could you identify them?"

"No," Paul said slowly. "It was . . . too dark. They had shaved heads, and wore, these, uh, choke chains like you'd put on a dog, but. . . ."

"Yeah, okay." The detective flipped open a notepad to write in it.

"Surveillance tape?" Paul said.

The detective glanced up. "Yeah, Mr. Bauhaus here has had so many problems, he had a camera installed on the building across the street aimed at his storefront. It caught the whole thing pretty well," he said, still writing.

Paul turned to Seth. "Your security guard was sleeping in the car."

"He'll be out the door as soon as I get hold of the company that sent him to us," Seth promised. "I'm sorry you got arrested, Paul. I didn't even know you were here until the detective called me this morning to watch the tape. And the minute I saw it, I knew that was you, puttin' your neck on the line for my business." Seth got a little emotional here, pausing to bring out his handkerchief and wipe his face.

"So I told the detective, 'That's Paul Arrendondo,' and he said you were here cooling your heels. I wish I could give you something for your trouble, but—the first time I forget to take the cash box home, I get cleaned out. The business will be closed for the next week for repairs, but then we'll be back better than ever. That sprinkler system will be in, and a high-dollar alarm system. I hope you can make that five hundred I gave you yesterday last until the insurance check comes."

"No problem, Seth," Paul said. He paused, debating whether to ask for a ride back to the warehouse. But, wary of explaining anything else—especially his tenancy in Streiker's warehouse—Paul decided he'd just foot it. It wasn't really that far.

The detective stopped writing to look at a young woman in a short skirt who had just entered in a rush, two people trailing her. She threw her purse on the intake counter and demanded, "Is Paul Arrendondo still here? I have his bail money!"

Upon hearing the voice, Paul turned in shock. "Royce?"

"Paul!" She ran over to throw herself on him and squeeze his neck. He held her in a stupor, then closed his eyes to relish the tightness of her grip. Meanwhile, Miriam and a preppy guy watched from the lobby. "Oh, Paul, why wouldn't you—"

Royce interrupted herself as the detective put his notepad away, revealing the badge on his belt. Thereupon she addressed him with controlled, feminine fury: "I don't know why you would arrest Paul for anything at all, but you are dead wrong about this. It's just ridiculous that anybody would accuse him of arson, and whoever said he did is lying through his teeth. My husband did not do this. You never met a straighter arrow in your life—you'll never know anybody who tries harder to do the right thing, even when—no, listen! If you'd just do a little more investigation instead of just locking up the first person you find—Paul is—he's just too good to do something like this!"

"Well," Detective Claussen said, "since you put it that way, I guess we'd better release him. You can take him and your bail money home."

Royce stared at him mistrustfully, but Seth reached out to shake Paul's hand. "I can't thank you enough, Paul. You stop by in a week, and we should be up and running by then."

"Sure, Seth," Paul said, shaking his hand.

Taking Royce's hand in bemused gratitude, Paul murmured, "Let's get out of here." He paused to ask Miriam, "Did you bring her?" and glanced at the man next to her.

"Bear did," she replied. "This is my fiancé, Dr. Beren."

"Hi," Paul said, extending his hand. "Uh, doctor—"

"Just Bear," he said cordially. "Yeah, I didn't want to miss this for anything."

They went outside to the sidewalk in the sunshine, and Royce looked down as Paul shifted on the hot concrete. "Well, no wonder you're shorter. What happened to your shoes?"

"I had to leave them. Long story. Royce—did you really bring five grand to bail me out?"

"Yes." She opened her purse to show him.

He caught his breath. "What're you—where did you get that? Streiker gave it to you! When did you talk to Streiker?"

"Fletcher Streiker? The Big Guy Upstairs?" Her eyes widened. "Good Lord, no. I've never talked to him. He wouldn't know me from Adam. Daddy wired me the money," she said, running a hand along his hard, delineated chest. "Wow, you're ripped," she murmured.

He started breathing a little harder, then looked down at the diamond—his diamond—that she wore on her ring finger. Blinking rapidly, he turned to the couple beside them. "Would you excuse us for just a second?"

"Sure." Miriam pulled her doctor bear a few feet away.

Paul turned back to Royce. "So—what does this mean for us? For you and me?"

"Oh, Paul," she exhaled, dropping her eyes. "I'm so sorry I blew you off. I want to stay married. I really do love you. That was so mean of you not to take my calls!" she cried.

"I lost my phone," he whispered, his eyes watering fiercely. "Royce, I . . . I'm flat broke. The position with the Streiker company never came through. I'm working at a real menial job, and even that's suspended for a week. I don't know. . . ."

"You know what?" she said. "I've always envied Buddy and Renetta for the traveling they do. Let's do that. Let's just take off—I don't care where—anywhere that we can earn a buck along the way. Just you and me, in that smelly old truck of yours."

"Do you mean that?" His voice cracked.

"Yes," she said, reaching up to kiss him. "You can listen to anything you want on the radio." She could not voice the dread "C" and "W" words. "Besides, I've got Daddy's five grand," she murmured into his lips.

He pulled away to walk her over to where Miriam and Bear were standing. "Thank you for bringing her down here. Would you mind running her back to wherever she got the wire?"

"Not at all," Doctor Bear said.

Royce began, "Paul—"

"I want you to wire that money right back to your dad and tell him it was all a misunderstanding," he said levelly. "My truck is not far. I'll get it and meet you back at your apartment."

"Let us drop you off at your truck," Bear offered, bringing out his keys.

"Thanks, no," Paul said hastily. He didn't want witnesses to his breaking into the warehouse. "I'd appreciate it if you'd just see that she gets the money wired back and gets home."

"We'll do that," Miriam purred, leaning over to stroke Paul's bristly chin. "And then Bear and I are going to be gone *for hours*." Paul grinned self-consciously, glancing at Royce, who was still caressing his pecs through his shirt.

He saw them off in Bear's BMW, then began gingerly trekking back to the warehouse over hot asphalt and litter-strewn medians. Along the way, he ruminated, *Wow. A surveillance camera. Well, sure, I should've known.* Yes, it made perfect sense, but he could hardly believe it. After reconciling himself to the fact of going to jail and losing everything, now all of a sudden he had Royce back. He had Seth's gratitude. He had his truck. He had his self-respect.

Yeah. He hopped over the concrete to walk in the grass, head up, looking around. He was mentally replaying the events of last night, trying to imagine how it would look on tape. *I'd sure like to see it—especially the part where I finally found the security guard.* He laughed out loud.

Royce wants me back. A warm glow covered him as

he replayed her passionate defense of him to the detective. She wasn't around last night; she couldn't have known anything about what happened. She only knew her husband. And she loved him. *Now that I know she feels that way, I can do anything for a living. It doesn't matter if I ever hear from Streiker again.*

Approaching the warehouse district, he looked over his shoulder to cross the street. Because his feet were burning and his heart was on fire, he ran the last few blocks to the warehouse. *Now, how to get back in? I'll have to break a window, if I can reach one.*

At the front of the warehouse, he paused to look around, shifting from foot to foot on the hot pavement. Being a hero and all, he wanted to make sure there were no witnesses to his intended crime. There was crime-scene tape all around the Bauhaus warehouse, and a fire marshal's truck out front, but no one outside that he could see.

He leaned over, wondering what the range of the security camera across the street might be. Then it occurred to him to maybe just try the door. Tentatively, Paul took hold of the old doorknob and turned. The door opened readily, and he walked on in, grateful for the cool concrete under his feet.

He glanced up across the warehouse and started. "Mr. Streiker."

15

Despite the distance from the door to the desk at the back, Paul recognized him immediately. Fletcher Streiker was sitting in the leather chair with his feet propped on the desk. Since Streiker did not react right away, Paul crossed the warehouse to see that he was reading his book. *The Aeneid.*

Respectfully, Paul waited until he put it down and looked up. "Good book," Fletcher observed. "I had forgotten what a good translation that is."

"I've really enjoyed it," Paul agreed. "I . . . thought you had gone to Hawaii."

"I came back."

"Just like that?" Paul wondered what he did about jet lag.

"I come and go just about however I please, Paul." With a mild grunt, Fletcher plopped his feet to the floor and shoved something across the desk toward Paul. "You need to call your mom."

"My phone!" Paul exclaimed, picking it up off the desk. "You found my phone!"

"No," Fletcher said. "You gave it to me."

"Gave it to you! What do you mean?"

"When you were unloading, you took it out of your pocket and handed it to me," Fletcher reminded him. As Paul stared at him, he added, "I didn't think you recognized me."

"You've had it all this time?" Paul asked. At Fletcher's nod, he demanded, "Why didn't you give it back to me?"

"Because I didn't think you needed it," Fletcher said coolly. Before Paul could vent indignant disagreement, Fletcher added, "You need it now. Call your mom."

"Well, I—" Flummoxed, Paul scrolled through the numbers to Jeannine's and pressed *talk*. Tightly, he added, "I would've checked on her before now, if I'd had my *phone*, but if you knew more about her, you'd know that she can't talk on a phone because she's—"

"Ferring residence," the line was answered. Dumbfounded at the voice, Paul did not speak, so the woman said, "Hello?"

"Mama?" he said, stricken.

"Paul? Is that you?" she said joyfully.

"Mama?" he cried. "How can you hear me?"

"Oh, Paul, Mrs. Ferring is so wonderful! She took me into San Angelo and got me hearing aids! For both ears! You would die if you knew how much they cost, but she wouldn't hear any talk of paying her back. I hear everything! Mostly. Oh, and this house, Paul! Is this not the most beautiful house you have ever seen? She lets me keep house! I can go into any room I want and clean. You should see my room! My very own room! With a *bathroom*, Paul. Right in the house!

"Oh, Paul—you left perfectly good jeans in the trash

can. I washed them and got the stain out. They're here for you next time you come. And I found your guitar, Paul. When you come, you can play it for me, and I will hear it. Won't that be nice?

"I can cook a decent dinner for you now! I go into town with Patricia—there's a wonderful little market where I can get whatever I want! The freshest of every-thing. They see me coming and say, 'Oh, it's Mrs. Ferring's household manager.' Isn't that something? as if I were somebody. I don't even have to pay—they put it 'on account.' And I get to cook whatever I want whenever I like—all the dishes that Papa loved! Even Patricia likes my cooking. . . . Paul?"

He was trying to stop crying. "That—that's great, Mama," he got out, wiping his eyes on his sleeve.

"Oh, Paul, Jeannine is here. She wants to talk to you," she said.

"Sure," he gulped.

"Paul? How are you? Have you found Royce?" Jeannine demanded.

"Yes, Jeannine, yeah, I'm doing great. Royce is—taking me back and we're going to make it work. You're getting a note soon that says differently, but she's taking me back."

"Oh, Paul, I'm so glad," she breathed.

He could tell that she meant it. "Jeannine, I can't thank you enough for what you did for Mama. I want to pay you for the hearing aids."

"Don't be ridiculous, Paul," she bristled. "It's the best investment I ever made. She does the work of three people—so I let Shana go. Juanita's a marvelous cook, and just a joy to be around. She sings while she's working, which is so comforting to listen to. It reminds me of Walt, the way he used to walk around whistling. I don't know how you turned out so glum, being raised by a mother like that."

"Just my nature," he laughed, again wiping his face fiercely.

"Speaking of Walt," she said in her voice of righteous vindication, "I was right. He remembered you."

"I'm sorry?" he said, uncomprehending.

"Roger finally got back to his office and found Walt's will. He left you the herd, Paul. So that sixty-eight thousand is yours."

"What?" he cried.

"What Joe Salinas paid for the herd is yours," she repeated.

He transferred the phone to his other ear. "Jeannine, I want you to take that money, and—"

"Oh, no," she interrupted. "I can't touch it. You'll just have to disburse it as you please whenever you come down."

"Okay," he exhaled. "I'll do that. Jeannine, I—have to go, but I'll—be down soon. Thank you again."

"You're welcome, Paul. Tell Royce hello."

"I will. Bye." He closed his phone, taking a minute to compose himself before looking up again.

Streiker was watching him. "You know that Aeneas achieved his destiny through obedience, Paul?"

"Yes," Paul said. "I know that. I haven't finished the book yet, but that much I remember. But—" he gestured helplessly, "what am I supposed to do? Mr. Harrison interviewed me, and I never heard back from him about the job, so I've been working next door, but I left notes, and he brought in the bed and the refrigerator, but—"

"Vince didn't do any of that," Fletcher corrected him.

"He didn't! Then who did?" Paul asked.

Fletcher cocked his head at Paul's ignorance. "I did."

"You—you were the one reading my notes?"

"Yes."

"But—what about Mr. Harrison?"

"He's long gone," Fletcher said.

"Gone! Where?"

"Promoted. He hired you as his replacement."

"Hired me? As president of Officina Gentium?" Paul cried.

"Yeees," Fletcher said with arched brow. "Didn't you get the key to your office?"

They both looked down at the warehouse key still sitting on the desk. "But—" Paul sputtered, "how—what was I supposed to do?"

"What you were doing," Fletcher said, rocking back in the chair. "I don't own Bauhaus, but Seth and I are on speaking terms, and he needed help getting his nephew Cam to step up to the plate and take his responsibilities with the company seriously."

At Paul's look of disbelief, Fletcher said, "Did you or did you not put on your application that you would do whatever I wanted you to do?"

"Yes."

"Well, that's what I wanted you to do."

"You mean, I'm through at Bauhaus?" Paul asked hopefully.

"Yes," Fletcher said.

"What do I do now?" Paul asked. "What the hell is Officina Gentium?"

"Workshop of the World, Paul. I have business interests all over the world, and I need people who are flexible enough to go where I tell them and do what I ask, even when they can't see the whole plan."

Paul stared at him. "Papa dying, and Jeannine taking Mama in . . . Mrs. Nicholas, and Bauhaus . . . the fire, and getting thrown in jail, and Royce coming to bail me out. . . . Who are you?" he breathed, awe gripping his heart.

There was an unreadable glint in Streiker's eye. "I am someone who is interested in you. And I am your boss."

"What makes you think I can do this job?" Paul asked in sudden apprehension.

"Let me ask you something." Fletcher leaned forward. "Was your heart's desire for Royce?"

Paul's eyes went to the middle distance so that he could look inward. It was imperative he give a fully truthful answer. "Not exactly," he finally allowed. "My heart's desire was to be the kind of man that she would want."

Fletcher swiveled back in the chair. "That's the kind of man who can do this job. So, how's your Spanish?"

"My Spanish?" Paul repeated blankly, and his face soured. He, like the rest of his siblings, had disassociated himself thoroughly from his heritage to escape the lingering effects of ingrained racism—such as the sergeant's assumption at processing. But while Streiker eyed him, Paul saw that this was part of the whole package that his boss was entitled to use at will. "*Mi español es bueno, señor.*"

"Good. You're going to need it where I'm sending you next, after you get back from San Angelo," Fletcher said, picking up the book again.

Paul hesitated while Fletcher started reading where he had left off. "What about Royce?" Paul asked with a twinge of fear. The dreaded choice between her and his calling loomed before him: Aeneas had lost his wife.

Fletcher glanced up. "Think she might want to go with you?"

Paul stared at him and then let down with a hazy grin. "Possibly." And there his identification with the great hero ended; having served his purpose, Aeneas slipped back into the spiritual world until such a time that he was needed again.

"Wellll?" Fletcher said leadingly.

"Well?" Paul repeated, snapping to.

"Don't you think you should go ask her?" Fletcher coaxed in mild exasperation.

"Go ask her. Yeah," Paul said, still smiling. He turned back toward the door.

"Paul."

"Yes?"

"Key." Fletcher held up the old-fashioned OG key.

"Oh, yeah." Abashed, Paul returned for the key, putting it in his jeans pocket. Then he turned back toward the door.

"Paul."

"Yes?"

"Boots." Fletcher eyed Paul's bare feet.

"Oh, man. Where is my brain at?" Paul sat on the

bed to don socks and boots, growing more excited by the moment. "You know, she just told me she wanted to travel."

"Really." Fletcher opened the book again.

"Yeah. Hey, how much will I make in this position?" Paul asked happily.

Fletcher looked at him over the book. "Will you trust me if I tell you it will be enough?"

"Yeah." Paul smiled in recognition of the second chance he was given to rely on Streiker's funding. With new urgency, he sprang up toward the door again.

"Paul!"

"Take the truck!" Paul shouted to himself, grabbing his wallet and remote from the desk. He opened the bay door, climbing into the truck to start it with a roar. As he screeched down the drive, he put the phone to his ear to listen to his missed messages.

Fletcher watched the bay door close again, then sighed, "Lord, what fools these mortals be." He smiled to himself, put his feet back up on the desk, and turned the page.

QUESTIONS TO HELP YOU GET THE MOST OUT OF THIS BOOK

1. Who is Fletcher Streiker?

2. Why is Fletcher dressed in a similar manner to Paul at their first meeting?

3. Why is Fletcher so hard on Paul?

4. How can Streiker say that everyone receives what they genuinely desire?

5. Why does a Christian book quote from mythology and talk about "gods"?

6. What does the employment application to Officina Gentium represent?

7. Who is Vince Harrison?

8. Why does Streiker keep Paul's phone?

9. What do Paul's notes to Harrison represent?

10. What is Officina Gentium?

11. Why doesn't Royce ever talk to Streiker?

The answers are currently in the Notes section of Robin's Facebook page. If you cannot locate them, contact her at mail@westfordpress.com.

Books by Robin Hardy

The Streiker Saga
Streiker's Bride
Streiker: The Killdeer
Streiker's Morning Sun

The Annals of Lystra
Chataine's Guardian
Stone of Help
Liberation of Lystra
(first published as *High Lord of Lystra*)

The Latter Annals of Lystra
Nicole of Prie Mer
Ares of Westford
Prisoners of Hope
Road of Vanishing
Dead Man's Token
Games of God and Men
In Extremis
All Mirrors and All Suns
The Laughing Side of the World

The Sammy Series
Sammy: Dallas Detective
Sammy: Women Troubles
Sammy: Working for a Living
Sammy: On Vacation
Sammy: Little Misunderstandings
Sammy: Ghosts
Sammy: Arenamania
Sammy: In Principle
(continued on next page)

Sammy: Grave Agreement
Sammy: Love Shouldn't Hurt
Sammy: The Consolation of Bucephalus

The Idecis
Unknown Name, Unknown Number: A Wimsey Reade Mystery
Padre and its sequel *His Strange Ways*

Edited by Robin Hardy

Sifted But Saved: Classic Devotions by W.W. Melton